Rachel was furious. She couldn't wait to put some distance between her and Nathan.

She rubbed the palm of her hand against her shorts. It was almost burning. The contact with his skin, the gentle feel of the hairs on his arms underneath her hand, was something she hadn't been ready for.

It was hard enough being around him again. She felt catapulted into a situation she was unprepared for. In her distant daydreams she'd been sure that if she ever met Nathan again she would be ready. Mentally. And physically.

She'd be wearing her best clothes. Something smart. Something professional. Her hair would be washed and her make-up freshly applied. She would have practised how to casually say hello. All her responses would be easy…nonchalant. Or at least rehearsed over and over again so they would seem that way.

She would have a five-minute conversation with him, wish him well for the future, and then walk off into the distance with a little swing of her hips.

She would be composed, controlled. He would never guess that her heart was breaking all over again. He would have no idea at all.

But most of all there would be absolutely no touching. *No touching at all.* Because in her head that had always been the thing that would break her.

And she'd been right.

Dear Reader,

What could be worse than being stranded on an island with your ex?

The short answer is—not much! And that's what happens to Rachel Johnson and Nathan Banks.

They parted company eight years before, and there's a lot for them to get through before they can finally reach their happy-ever-after.

I had great fun writing this book. Rachel and Nathan have the pleasure of being the medical crew on a fictional TV show. Both of them are doing a favour for a mutual friend who hasn't let either of them know the other is going to be there. Sparks certainly fly!

I love to hear from readers. You can find me at scarlet-wilson.com, on Facebook, and on Twitter as @scarlet_wilson.

Hope you enjoy!

Scarlet

THE DOCTOR
SHE LEFT BEHIND

BY
SCARLET WILSON

First published in Great Britain 2015
by Mills & Boon, an imprint of Harlequin (UK) Limited,
Large Print edition 2016
Eton House, 18-24 Paradise Road,
Richmond, Surrey TW9 1SR

© 2015 Scarlet Wilson

ISBN: 978-0-263-26070-0

Harlequin (UK) Limited's policy is to use papers that are natural, renewable and recyclable products and made from wood grown in sustainable forests. The logging and manufacturing processes conform to the legal environmental regulations of the country of origin.

Printed and bound in Great Britain
by CPI Antony Rowe, Chippenham, Wiltshire

Scarlet Wilson wrote her first story aged eight and has never stopped. Her family have fond memories of *Shirley and the Magic Purse*, with its army of mice all with names beginning with the letter 'M'. An avid reader, Scarlet started with every Enid Blyton book, moved on to the *Chalet School* series and many years later found Mills & Boon.

She trained and worked as a nurse and health visitor, and currently works in public health. For her, finding Mills & Boon Medical Romance was a match made in heaven. She is delighted to find herself amongst the authors she has read for many years.

Scarlet lives on the West Coast of Scotland with her fiancé and their two sons.

Books by Scarlet Wilson

Mills & Boon Medical Romance

Rebels with a Cause
The Maverick Doctor and Miss Prim
About That Night...

The Boy Who Made Them Love Again
West Wing to Maternity Wing!
A Bond Between Strangers
Her Christmas Eve Diamond
An Inescapable Temptation
Her Firefighter Under the Mistletoe
200 Harley Street: Girl from the Red Carpet
A Mother's Secret
Tempted by Her Boss
Christmas with the Maverick Millionaire

Visit the Author Profile page at
millsandboon.co.uk for more titles.

For Cathy McAuliffe, Catherine Bain and
Shirley Bain with lots of love for the women
who manage to put up with all these Bain boys!

Praise for
Scarlet Wilson

'*Her Christmas Eve Diamond* is a fun and
interesting read. If you like a sweet romance
with just a touch of the holiday season you'll
like this one.'

—*HarlequinJunkie*

'*West Wing to Maternity Wing!* is a tender,
poignant and highly affecting romance that is
sure to bring a tear to your eye. With her gift
for creating wonderful characters, her ability
to handle delicately and compassionately
sensitive issues and her talent for writing
believable, emotional and spellbinding
romance, the talented Scarlet Wilson continues
to prove to be a force to be reckoned with in
the world of contemporary romantic fiction!'

—*CataRomance*

CHAPTER ONE

'YOU REALLY THINK this is a good idea?' Nathan Banks shook his head. Nothing about this sounded like a good idea to him.

But Lewis nodded. 'I think it's a great idea. I need a doctor. You need a job.'

'But I already have a job.' He lifted his hands. 'At least I think I do. Is my contract not being renewed?'

His stomach turned over a little. Last night had been a particularly bad night in A & E. His medical skills were never in question but his temper had definitely been short. It hadn't been helped by hearing a car backfire on the walk home and automatically dropping to the ground as if it were gunfire. His last mission for Doctors Without Borders had been in a war zone. Dropping to the floor when you heard gunfire had become normal for him. But doing it in the streets of Melbourne? Not his proudest moment. Particularly when a kid on the way to school had asked him what was wrong.

Lewis smiled. The way he always did when he was being particularly persuasive. Nathan had learned to spot it over the years. 'The last few days in A & E have been tough. You came straight out of Doctors Without Borders after five years and started working here. You've never really had a holiday. Think of this as your lucky day.'

Nathan lifted the buff-coloured folders. 'But this isn't a holiday. This is a form of torture. My idea of a holiday is walking in the hills of Scotland somewhere, or surfing on Bondi Beach. Being stranded on an island with nine B-list celebrities? I'm the least celeb-orientated person on the planet. I couldn't care less about these people.'

Lewis nodded. 'Exactly. That's what makes you perfect. You can be objective. All you need to do is supervise the fake TV challenges and monitor these folk's medical conditions for the three weeks they're on the island. The rest of the

time you'll get to sit around with your feet up.'
He bent over next to Nathan and put one hand
on his shoulder, waving the other around as if he
were directing a movie. 'Think of it—the beautiful Whitsunday islands, the surrounding Coral
Sea, luxury accommodation and perfect weather
with only a few hours' work a day. What on earth
could go wrong?'

Nathan flipped open the first folder. Everything
about this seemed like a bad idea. It was just a
pity that the viewing public seemed to think it
was a great one. *Celebrity Island* had some of the
best viewing figures on the planet. 'But some of
these people shouldn't be going to a celebrity island, let alone doing any challenges. They have
serious medical conditions.'

Lewis waved his hand. 'And they've all had
million-dollar medicals for the insurance company. The TV company needs someone with A
& E experience who can think on their feet.'

'I hardly think epidemic, natural disaster and
armed conflict experience is what a TV crew
needs.'

Lewis threw another folder towards him. 'Here.

Read up on snake bites, spiders and venom. The camp will be checked every night but you can't be too careful.'

The expression on Lewis's face changed. The hard sell wasn't working and it was obvious he was getting desperate.

'Please, Nathan. I agreed to this contract before I knew Cara was pregnant. I need to find someone to replace me on the island. The last thing I want is to end up sued for breach of contract. You're the one person I trust enough to ask.'

Nathan took a long, slow breath. Working for a TV company was the last thing he wanted to do. But Lewis was right. He was close to burnout. And in some ways he was lucky his friend had recognised it. How bad could three weeks on an island in the Coral Sea be? The celebs might have to sleep by a campfire but the production crew were supposed to have luxury accommodation. He shook his head. 'Why didn't you just tell me this was about Cara's pregnancy?'

Lewis looked away for a second. 'There have been a few issues. A few complications—a few hiccups as we've got closer to the end. We didn't really want to tell anyone.' He slid something over the desk towards him. 'Here, the final sweetener. Look at the pay cheque.'

Nathan's eyes boggled. 'How much?' He shook his head again. 'It doesn't matter what the pay cheque is, if you'd told me this was about Cara I would have said yes right away.' He lifted his hands. 'I would have volunteered and done it for nothing. Sometimes you've got to be straight with people, Lewis.'

Lewis blinked, as if he was contemplating saying something else. Then he gave his head a little shake. 'Thank you, Nathan.' He walked around and touched Nathan's shoulder. 'I need a medic I can trust. You'll have back-up. Another doctor is flying out from Canberra to join the TV crew too. Last year I was there I worked twelve hours—tops—over three weeks. Trust me. This will be the easiest job you've ever had.'

Nathan nodded slowly. It still didn't appeal. He had a low tolerance to all things celebrity. But three weeks of easy paid work in a luxury location? He'd have to be a fool to say no. Plus, Lewis had helped him when he'd landed in Australia straight out of Doctors Without Borders and with no job. Of course he'd help. 'What happens when I get back?'

Lewis met his gaze. 'You're a great medic. We're lucky to have you. I'll give you another six-month contract for A & E—if you want it, of course.'

He hesitated only for a second. Lewis was one of his oldest friends and he knew they'd waited four years for Cara to fall pregnant. There was no way he could let him down. Even if it was the last place on this earth he wanted to go.

He picked up the pen. 'Tell Cara I'll be thinking about her. Okay, where do I sign?'

Rachel Johnson took a few final moments lying on the sun lounger at the pool. She couldn't believe for a second she was getting paid for this.

She'd been here two days and hadn't had to do a minute of work. Apparently her job started as soon as she hit the island. Which was fine by her. From what she'd seen of the nine celebrities taking part in *Celebrity Island,* she suspected they ranged from mildly whiny to difficult and impossible. Her old university friend Lewis Blake had persuaded her to take part and the fee was astronomical. But that wasn't why she was here.

She was here because her Hippocratic oath seemed to have her over a barrel. Her ex—an Australian soap star—was taking part. And she was one of the few that knew his real medical history. It seemed that one of his bargaining chips had been to ask for a doctor he could trust. And even though there was nothing between them, part of her felt obliged to help.

'Are you ready, Dr Johnson? The seaplane has just landed.'

Rachel jumped up from the comfortable lounger and grabbed her rucksack packed with her clothes. Two days staying in the luxury five-star resort had been bliss. All the medical supplies she would need had already been shipped. Apparently the other medic was already on the island. And since there was no way off the island for the next three weeks she hoped it was someone she could work with. Between the two of them, they would be on call twenty-four hours a day for three weeks. Lewis had assured her that apart from monitoring the challenges there really wasn't anything to do. But, as much as she loved him, Lewis had always been economical with the truth.

Rachel climbed into the seaplane that was bobbing on the blue ocean. She'd never been in one of these before and the ride was more than a little bumpy. But the view over the island worth it.

The pilot circled the island, letting her see the full geography. 'This is the beach where some of the celebrities will be dropped off. The beach on the other side is for the crew. It has umbrellas, sun loungers and a bar—so don't worry, you'll be well looked after.' As he crossed the middle of the island the view changed to a thick jungle. 'Camp is in the middle,' he said. 'Don't tell anyone but they actually have a rain canopy they can pull overhead if we get one of the seasonal downpours. We didn't have it the first year and the whole camp got swept away in a torrent of water.'

Rachel shifted uncomfortably in her seat. That sounded a little rougher than she'd expected. 'Where will I be staying?'

He pointed to some grey rectangular buildings in the distance. 'The three big grey buildings are the technical huts and production gallery. You'll be staying in a portable cabin. The medical centre is right next to you.' He let out a laugh that sounded more like a pantomime witch's cackle. 'Just next to the swamp and the rope bridge. The celebrities love those.' He gave Rachel a nod. 'I won't tell you how many of them have fallen off that rope bridge.'

For a second her throat felt dry. Lewis's version of the truth was already starting to unravel. A portable cabin and a hotel were not the same thing. Her dreams of a luxury bed and state-of-the-art facilities had just vanished in the splutter of a seaplane's engines. There might be an ocean right next to her but there was no swimming pool, no facilities and definitely no room service. This was sounding less and less like three weeks in the sun and more and more like she would be wringing Lewis's neck the next time she saw him.

The seaplane slowed and bumped to a landing on the water, moving over to a wooden quay. A burly man in a grey T-shirt tinged with sweat grabbed the line so she could open the door and jump down.

'Doc Johnson?'

She nodded.

He rolled his eyes. 'I'm Ron. Welcome to paradise.'

The wooden quay gave a little sway as she landed on it.

They walked quickly along the beach and up a path towards the grey portable cabins. 'Kind of out of place for paradise?' she said.

Ron laughed. 'Is that how they got you out here? Told the same story to the other doc too. But he's been fine. Said he's used to sleeping in camp beds anyhow and it doesn't make any difference to him.'

A horrible shiver crept down Rachel's spine. She'd spent five years at university in London with Lewis and a group of other friends. Then another couple of years working in the surrounding London hospitals. Lewis knew everything about her. He knew everything about the guy she'd dated for five years back then. Lewis was the common denominator here. He wouldn't have done anything stupid, would he?

Ron showed her up to the three cabins sitting on an incline. 'The rest of the crew stay along the beach a little. You and the other doc are in here. Medical centre is right next to you. And the one next to that is the most popular cabin on the beach.'

'Showers?' she said hopefully.

'Nope. Catering,' he answered with a broad smile.

'Okay. Thanks, Ron.' She pushed open the door to the cabin and sent a silent prayer upwards.

The cabin was empty. There was a sitting area in the middle with a sofa. A bathroom with a shower of sorts, and two rooms at either end. It wasn't quite army camp beds. They were a little better than that. But the rooms were sparse, with only a small chest of drawers and a few hooks on the wall with clothes hangers on them.

Rachel dumped her rucksack and washed her face and hands, taking a few minutes to change her T-shirt and apply some more mosquito spray and sunscreen.

Her stomach was doing little flip-flops. It was pathetic really. Ron had only made one remark about a camp bed. It was nothing. It could apply to millions of guys the world over. But she had a bad feeling about this. Lewis had been especially persuasive on the phone. He'd given her the whole 'my wife is pregnant' and 'one of the celebrities is being difficult' routine. When she'd heard who the celebrity was she hadn't been surprised. She'd met Darius under unusual circumstances. Both of them had been vulnerable. And he'd loved the thought that by dating a doctor he had an insider's view of treatments.

But dating Darius Cornell—Australia's resident soap opera hunk—had been an experience. They'd dated for just over a year. Just enough to get both of them through. She'd been relieved when the media attention had died down.

Her stomach flipped over one more time as she walked outside and reached for the door handle of the medical centre. It was strange to be here at his request. But Darius could be handled.

Her biggest fear was that the person behind this door probably couldn't.

* * *

He was dreaming. More likely he was having a nightmare. He pushed his hat a little further back on his head and blinked again.

No. She was still there.

Rachel Johnson. Brown hair tied in a ponytail, slightly suntanned skin and angry brown eyes set off by her pink T-shirt.

'Just when I thought this couldn't get any worse.' He pulled his feet off the desk.

Her lips tightened and her gaze narrowed. 'I'm going to kill Lewis Blake. I'm going to kill him with my bare hands. There's no way I'm getting stuck on this island with you for three weeks.' She folded her arms across her chest.

He pointed out at the sky. 'Too late, Rach. You just missed your ride home.' The seaplane was heading off in the distance.

Her forehead creased into a deep frown. 'No way. There must be a boat. Another island nearby. How do they get supplies?'

Nathan shrugged. 'Not sure. I've only been here a day. And don't worry. I'm just as happy to see you. Particularly when I've just looked through the medical notes and saw your lovely ex is one of the celebs. No wonder you're here.'

He couldn't help it. When they'd split up years ago Rachel had come to Australia and a few months later been photographed by the press with her new boyfriend—an Australian soap star. It had been hard enough to get over the split, but seeing his ex all over the press when he'd been left behind to take care of his younger brother had just rubbed salt in the wounds. *She'd* gone to Australia. The place they'd planned to go to together.

'What exactly are you doing here, Nathan? You seem the last person who'd want a job like this.'

He raised his eyebrows. 'And what's that supposed to mean?'

She shrugged. 'I'd heard you were working for Doctors Without Borders. *Celebrity Island* seems a bit of a stretch of the imagination.'

He tried to ignore the little surge of pleasure that sparked; she'd been interested enough to find out where he worked. He'd never wanted to ask any of their mutual friends where Rachel was. Everyone knew that she'd gone to Australia without him and they were much too tactful to bring up her name.

He folded his arms across his chest. 'I think you know exactly why I'm here. At a guess I'd say he hoodwinked me just as much as he hoodwinked you.' He gave his hands a little rub together. 'But don't worry. I've got three weeks to think of what I'll do to him when I get back.'

She frowned again. 'How did he get in touch?'

Nathan's gaze met hers. 'I've been working with him.'

'In A & E?'

Nathan shrugged. 'Seemed the most logical place to work after five missions with Doctors Without Borders. He offered me the job as soon as my feet hit Australian soil.'

She gave a little nod. He could almost hear her brain ticking. He'd been the logical one and she'd been the emotional one. He'd thought they'd counterbalanced each other and worked well together. He'd been wrong.

'And don't think I've not noticed.'

Her cheeks were flooded with colour. 'Noticed what?' she snapped.

'That there's information missing from his medical file. What does your boyfriend have to hide?'

'Stop calling him that. He's not my boyfriend. Hasn't been for more than seven years. It might have escaped your notice but he's actually engaged to someone else. There's absolutely nothing between us.' She was getting angrier and angrier as she spoke. The colour was rushing up her face to the tips of her ears. He'd forgotten how mad she could get about things. Particularly when something mattered to her.

He lifted up the nearest folder. It took both hands. 'Look at this one.'

She frowned and placed her hands on her hips. 'Who does that belong to?'

'Diamond Dazzle. Model. Grand old age of twenty-two and look at the size of her medical records. I know every blood test, every X-ray and every piece of plastic surgery and Botox she's ever had. This one?' He held up Darius's records. Paper-thin. 'I know that Darius had an appendectomy at age eight. That's it.'

She folded her arms across her chest. 'And that's all you need to know. I know the rest.'

'No physician works like that, Rach.'

'You work like that every day, Nathan. You rarely know the history of the people who turn up in A & E, and I imagine on your missions you must have had patients from everywhere. They didn't come with medical files.'

He stood up. She was annoying every part of him now. It didn't matter that the angrier and more stubborn she got—the more her jaw was set—the more sensations sparked around his body. Rachel had always had this effect on him. He'd just expected it would have disappeared over time and with a whole host of bad memories. The rush of blood around his system was definitely unwelcome. 'So, you're going to look after one patient and I'll look after eight? Is that how we're going to work things?'

She shook her head fiercely, her eyes flashing. Rachel had always hated it when someone suggested she didn't pull her weight. After all these years he still knew what buttons to press.

'No, Nathan. I'll look after *all* the patients—just like you will—if required.'

But Nathan wouldn't be beaten. Not after all these years. He folded his own arms across his chest and matched Rachel's stance. He couldn't help but smile. It was like a stand-off. 'Well, I don't think I can do that if I don't have all the facts about the patient.'

The colour of her face practically matched her T-shirt now and he could see tiny beads of sweat on her brow. It was unquestionably hot on the island. But he was quite sure that wasn't why Rachel Johnson was sweating.

She shifted her feet. It was unusual to see her in khaki shorts, thick socks and heavy boots. She'd obviously been warned about the island paths. Rachel had spent her time as a student and junior doctor dressed smartly. Always in dresses and heels. This was a whole new look for her. Maybe her time in Australia had changed her outlook on life?

'Of course you can, Nathan. Stop being difficult. Three weeks. I can tell you'll be scoring off the days on the calendar just like I will.'

She turned to walk away. And it surprised him just how much he actually didn't want her to. If you'd asked him if he wanted to come face to face with Rachel Johnson again he'd have said, *Not in this lifetime*. But reality was sometimes stranger than fiction.

She stopped at the door. 'How's Charlie?'

The question caught him off guard and his answer was an automatic response. 'Charlie's fine. Not that you would care.'

She sighed. 'That's not fair, Nathan, and you know it.'

He shrugged. 'Why? You didn't want to hang around when I had to look after my little brother for a couple of years. Why bother now?'

She shook her head. He could see her biting her lip. She probably couldn't find the words for why she'd run out on them both. 'I always loved Charlie. He was great. Did he finish university?' A thought must have flickered across her mind. 'How was he when you were away?'

'Charlie was fine. He finished his engineering degree and got a job before I left for my last mission. He's married now with two young children.'

She gave a little nod of her head. 'Glad to hear it. Tell him I'm asking for him.'

She walked out of the door, letting it slam behind her. Nathan picked up the bottle of water on the table and downed it in one, wishing it was a beer. No matter how he tried to avoid it, his eyes had settled on her backside and legs as she'd walked out of the door. Eight years on and Rachel Johnson was as hot as ever.

And eight years later she still drove him crazy.

I always loved Charlie. The words echoed in his mind. 'Just as well you loved one of us,' he muttered.

She'd thought the cabin was hot but outside was even hotter and the high humidity was making the sweat trickle down her back already, probably turning her hair into a frizz bomb.

She stopped for a second to catch her breath, leaning against the metal bodywork and hoping to feel a little of the coolness on her body.

Trapped on an island with two exes. You couldn't make this up.

A little wave of nausea rolled over her. Nathan

Banks. Eight years had done nothing to diminish the impact of seeing him again. Her hands were trembling and every hair on her arms stood on end. She'd never expected to come face-to-face with him again.

His blond hair was a little shorter. His build a bit more muscular. But his eyes were still the neon green they'd always been. They could stop any girl in her tracks—just like they'd done to her.

They were supposed to be continents apart. What on earth was he doing in Australia? She knew he'd spent five years working for Doctors Without Borders. He was still friends with a lot of the people they'd trained with. And even though she'd pretended not to, she'd spent the last five years searching mutual social media sites with her heart in her mouth, hoping she wouldn't ever hear bad news about him. That was the trouble with working in humanitarian missions—sometimes they took you into places with armed conflict.

Trouble was, five minutes in Nathan's company could make her *mad*. No one else in her life had ever managed to spark that kind of reaction from her. But there was just something about Nathan and her alone in a room together. Sparks always flew. Sometimes good. Sometimes bad.

It was clear he still hadn't forgiven her for leaving. She couldn't blame him. But if she'd told him why she was really leaving he would have put his life—and Charlie's—on hold for her. She hadn't wanted that—she couldn't do that to them. They'd just lost their parents; they'd needed to focus on each other.

And if she told him now why she'd left, she would be betraying Darius's trust. Caught between the devil and the deep blue sea.

She stared out at the perfect blue Coral Sea. It was no wonder they'd picked one of the Whitsunday islands for this show. At any other time, with any other person, this would be perfect.

Too bad Nathan Banks was here to spoil it for her.

CHAPTER TWO

'EXACTLY HOW LONG will this take?' The director was scowling at them both.

Nathan shrugged. He couldn't care less about the man's bad attitude. 'It'll take as long as it takes. We need to see every participant and have a quick chat about their medical history—then we'll be able to tell you if anyone is unsuitable for the challenge tomorrow.'

The director stomped out of the door, closing it with an exasperated bang.

Nathan smiled at Rachel. 'Now, where were we?'

Rachel lifted the printed list. 'Okay, we have nine celebrities and one backup that we'll need to assess if he arrives.' She frowned. 'This doesn't seem right. Aren't they all supposed to be filmed jumping from a plane and rowing or snorkelling their way here? What are they doing already on the island?'

Nathan shrugged. 'The magic of television. They arrived yesterday when I did. They plan to do the filming later on today, pretending they've just set foot on the island. But they haven't seen the camp yet. They spent last night in one of the cabins and you want to have heard the list of complaints.'

She shook her head as she looked over the list. 'More fool me. I had no idea they faked their arrival. Want to take a bet on how quickly one will bail?'

He held out his fist. Old habits died hard. He and Rachel used to do this all the time. She blinked as if she were having a little flash of memory, then held out her fist, bumping it against his. 'Six days.'

He shook his head. 'Oh, way too ambitious. Four days.'

She frowned. 'Really? But they're doing it for charity. Surely someone wouldn't give up that easy?'

He raised his eyebrows. 'You really think these people are doing it all just for charity?'

'Of course.' She looked confused and Nathan sighed and picked up the list.

'Let's see. Darius Cornell—actor—let's leave him for now. Diamond Dazzle—model—she's looking for a lingerie contract. Frank Cairns—sportsman—he's looking for a presenter's job somewhere. Molly Bates—comedienne—she needs the publicity for her upcoming tour. Tallie Turner—actress—she just needs a job. Pauline Wilding—politician—always likes to be in the papers. Fox—boy band pop star—he's hoping some teenagers remember his crazy name. Billy X—rapper—with his past history he's probably about to be arrested for something, and Rainbow Blossom—reality TV star. She probably doesn't want to fade from the spotlight. Are any of these people actually celebrities? Do any of them have a real name?'

He saw Rachel's lips press together and waited for her to immediately go on the offensive for her apparent ex. But she surprised him. She didn't.

'I didn't realise you were such a cynic.'

'I guess we really didn't know each other at all, did we?' he shot back.

The words hung in the air between them. He sounded bitter. And he was. But even he was surprised by how quickly the words had come out. They'd never had this conversation before. She'd just told him she was leaving and hotfooted it out of the hospital as if she were being chased by a bunch of killer zombies.

Five years of missions for Doctors Without Borders had loosened his tongue. He'd dealt with armed conflict, natural disasters and epidemics. He was less willing to placate and tolerate. Life was too short—he knew that now. He and his brother had lost their parents to an accident eight years ago, and he'd lost too many patients all over the world.

She flopped down into the chair next to him, letting her floral scent drift under his nose. That was new. Rachel didn't smell like that before. She'd always worn something lighter. This was stronger, more sultry, more like something a woman eight years on would wear. Why would he expect anything to stay the same?

'Actually, you're right,' she muttered, going back to the original conversation and completely

ignoring his barb. 'Darius is probably the most
well-known of them all. Five of them I don't recognise and three I've never even heard of.'

It was almost a relief that finally they could
agree on something.

'How do you want to do this?' She pointed to
the pile of notes. 'Do you want to go over each
patient individually or do you just want to split
them up?'

Splitting the pile would be easier and quicker.
But Nathan wasn't about to let her off so easy.
He needed to have another doctor he could rely
on. Rachel had been a good doctor eight years
ago—but he'd no idea how she was now. 'Let's
do them together. That way, if either of us is on
call we're familiar with all the patients. There's
only nine—this won't take too long.'

He picked up the nearest set of notes and started
flicking. 'Diamond Dazzle—real name Mandy
Brooks. She's had liposuction, two breast en-
largements, one skin biopsy, one irregular smear
test and lots of Botox. She apparently had her lips
done a week ago—so we'll need to keep an eye
on her for any signs of infection.'

Rachel shook her head. 'Why would an already beautiful twenty-two-year-old think she needs all this?'

Nathan put the file back on the desk. 'Beats me.' He folded his arms across his chest. 'Do you think this makes her ineligible for the challenge? Having spiders or rats crawl over her body—and probably face too—will make her more vulnerable to infection.'

'I think just being in the jungle alone makes her at higher risk. Who would do that? Know that they're coming somewhere like this and go for a procedure less than a week before?'

Nathan smiled. He knew exactly where she was coming from but he also knew the answer. 'Someone who wants to be on TV.'

Rachel shook her head. Some of her hair was coming loose and the curls were starting to stray around her face. It was odd. She hadn't aged as much as he had. There were a few tiny lines around her eyes and her body had filled out a little. But nothing else. She was every bit as beautiful as he remembered.

His face and skin had been weathered by five

years of on and off postings in countries around the world. The last had been the worst. The sand felt as if it would never wash off and the darkening of his skin—coupled with lots of lines—made him more weathered. It didn't help that he felt about a hundred years older.

'Shall we call her in?' He had to focus on work. That was what they were here to do. Lewis hadn't lied about everything. On the surface, this could be three weeks of paid vacation time. Supervising the challenges would only take a couple of hours each night. He could live with that.

Rachel stood up and walked to the door. 'I'll get her. They're down on the beach with the director. Apparently they're going to make it look like they had to row part way here.'

Nathan just rolled his eyes.

It didn't take long to chat to each celebrity and review their medical files. A few were taking medications that they'd still require in the camp. A few others had intermittent usage of medications for angina, migraines or asthma that Rachel and Nathan agreed they could still take into camp. None of that stuff would be shown on camera.

Eventually it was time to speak to Darius. As soon as the guy walked into the room Nathan bristled. He just didn't like him—would never like him. For some reason, the pictures of Darius and Rachel together were imprinted on his brain.

Rachel smiled nervously. 'Darius, this is Nathan, the other doctor on duty. We are having a chat with everyone about their medical file and requirements in the camp.'

Darius had that soap actor look. Clean tanned skin and straight white teeth. He looked as if on occasion he might work out at the gym and he also looked as if he needed to gain a little weight.

Nathan held up his file as Rachel shifted from foot to foot. 'There's not much in here, Darius. If I'm going to be the doctor looking after you I need to know a little more about your medical history.'

Darius's eyes shifted over to Rachel. He was a confident guy who was obviously used to things going his way. 'There's no need. Rachel knows my medical history. That's why she's here.'

Nathan leaned across the desk. 'But Rachel might not always be available. She's not on call twenty-four hours a day for the next three weeks, you know. And she'll have other patients to treat too. The rest of your campmates and the crew need doctor services too.'

Darius gave a fake smile as he glanced at Rachel. 'I'm sure she'll cope.'

Nathan's hand balled into a fist as he kept his voice deadly calm. 'Any allergies I should know about? Are you in good health right now? Do you require any medications or special diet requirements?'

Darius took a few seconds to reply, almost as if he was rehearsing his answer. 'No allergies. I'm in perfect health and I'm not taking any medication right now.'

Measured. That was the word that Nathan would use. Rachel, in comparison, looked like a cat on a hot tin roof. What on earth had happened between these two?

There was something in the air. But it wasn't like the spark Nathan had felt between him and her when Rachel had first walked in here. It was something different. Something easier—at least it seemed easier to Darius. He seemed cool and confident around Rachel. Assured.

Darius stood up and put a hand on Rachel's shoulder. 'Thanks for being here, Rach.' He glanced at Nathan. 'I hope it doesn't cause you too many problems.'

He disappeared out of the door to where the director was assembling the production crew.

Nathan folded his arms. 'Well, that was informative. What does he have on you, Rach?'

Her expression of relief changed quickly. It was amazing how quickly he could put her back up. 'What do you mean? Nothing. He has nothing on me. Why would you even think that? I've already told you I'll be looking after Darius. There's nothing you need to know.' She was getting angrier by the second and he knew he was right.

He moved around the desk, leaning back against it, only inches away from where she stood. Her perfume filled the air around him. 'Really? So what did he mean by "I'm not taking any medication *right now*"? When was he taking meds and what for?'

He could see the conflict flitting across her eyes. The rational part of her brain knew exactly why he was asking. His suspicion hadn't been misplaced. There was something to tell; that was the whole reason Rachel was here. But what was it? Three weeks of this would drive him crazy.

She stared him straight in the eye. 'This is ridiculous. I don't want to be here. You don't want to be here. Why doesn't one of us just leave?'

She was cutting straight to the chase but he hadn't missed the fact she'd just circumvented his question.

This was the closest he'd been to Rachel in eight long years. Her pink lips were pressed in a hard line and her hands were staunchly on her hips. He tried not to look down. He tried not to notice the way her breasts were straining against the thin pink T-shirt. He tried not to notice the little lines around her brown eyes. Or the faint tan on her unblemished skin.

But everything was there. Everything was right in front of him. He breathed in and her scent was like an assault on his senses. He bristled, the tiny hairs on his skin upright and the beat of his heart increasing in his chest. This was crazy. He wasn't interested in this woman. He wouldn't *let* himself be interested in this woman. She'd walked away. More accurately, she'd flown away when he and Charlie had needed her most.

Australia hadn't just been her dream. It had been *their* dream. They'd both planned on going there after they'd worked as senior house doctors for a year. It was easier for Rachel. Her mother was Australian and Rachel had dual nationality. But the application to work had been in both of their names and nothing had hurt more than when Rachel had just upped and left without him.

The words were on the tip of his tongue. *You leave.* But he couldn't bring himself to say them. And it drove him crazy. It should be easy. She deserved it. So why couldn't he say it?

He turned his back and sat back down. He had to get away from her smell, her stance, the look in her eyes. He could do without all these memories.

'I can't leave. I'm working with Lewis. Believe it or not, I'm doing this as a favour to him. Cara's near the end of her pregnancy and he needs to be there. When I go back he'll give me another six-month contract at the hospital.'

She frowned, wrinkling her nose. Rachel had always looked cute when she was frowning. 'He's blackmailing you into being here?' It sounded worse when she said it out loud.

He couldn't help the rueful smile on his face. 'Not really. He gave me "the look". You know— the one he always gives you when he needs his own way? Anyway, he really didn't want to be away from Cara and apparently I needed a holi-day. A break. Some time off.'

Now she looked worried. 'He thought you needed some time off? Is something wrong? Did something happen?'

You. But he'd never say that word out loud. He hadn't realised how big an effect all this was hav-ing on him. And he didn't even want to acknowl-edge it. He'd spent the last eight years blanking Rachel out of his life. Forgetting about her. Lock-ing her away in a box, along with all the unre-solved feelings he had about her. It wasn't quite so easy to do that when she was standing in front of him.

He took the easy route. 'I spent five years working for Doctors Without Borders. I've been halfway around the world. I didn't really have a holiday when I finished my last tour. Just came to Australia, looked up Lewis and started working for him on a temporary contract.'

She hesitated, something flitting across her eyes. 'You never talked about going to Doctors Without Borders. What made you go?'

He couldn't bite back his natural response. 'We didn't talk about lots of things.'

She flinched, almost as if she'd been stung.

He took a deep breath. 'An old friend came back after working for them. When he told me about the work he'd been doing—the epidemics, the natural disasters and in areas of armed conflict—I was interested. Who wouldn't be? Lots of these people have absolutely no access to healthcare. Doctors Without Borders is their only hope. I felt as if I had to go. Charlie had finished university and got a job. The timing worked out. I was only going to do one mission in Africa for nine months. But one year turned into two, then three and eventually five.'

He paused. She was watching him carefully, almost holding her breath. 'It was good experience.' It seemed the best way to sum things up. Rachel didn't need to know what he'd seen or what he'd dealt with. She had a good enough imagination. He'd already told her more than he'd intended to.

But curiosity about her was getting the better of him. 'What's your speciality?'

For a second she seemed thrown. She bit her lip and fixed her eyes on a spot on the wall, her hand tugging nervously at her ear.

With Rach, it had always been a telltale sign. And his instant recognition came like a thunderbolt. He'd thought he'd known this woman so well. But he hadn't really known her at all. That was probably what stung the most.

'I took a little time off when I came to Australia.' Her eyes looked up to the left. 'Then I worked as a general medical physician for a while, dealing with a mix of diabetic, cardiac, respiratory and oncology patients.' Her feet shifted on the floor.

Her gaze meshed with his and something shot

through him. A wave of recognition. She tugged at her ear. *She's going to change the subject.*

After all these years he still knew her little nuances. 'I thought you might have gone into surgery. That's what you were always interested in.'

She was right. He had talked about going into surgery. And he'd certainly had his fair share of surgical experience around the world. But even though he'd just acknowledged that he still knew her little nuances, he was annoyed that she thought she still knew things about him.

She'd walked away. She'd lost the right to know anything about him. She'd lost the right to have any insight into his life.

His voice was blunt. 'A surgical internship would have taken up too many hours. At least with A & E I had regular shifts without also being on call.'

The implication was clear. Looking after his brother had changed his career pathway. He didn't like to think about it. He didn't like to acknowledge it—especially not to someone who had turned and walked away. Maybe if Rachel had stayed he could still have chosen surgery as his path? It would have been easier to share the load between two people.

But Rachel didn't seem to be picking up his annoyance. 'You must have got a wide range of experience with Doctors Without Borders. Did you do some surgery?'

'Of course I did. It's all hands on deck out there, even though you're in the middle of the desert.' His eyes drifted off to the grey wall. If he closed his eyes right now he could almost hear the whump-whump of the incoming medevac helicopters. He could feel the sensation of the tiny hairs on his arms and at the back of his neck standing on end in nervous anticipation of the unknown.

Sometimes civilians—men, women and children—sometimes army, navy or air force personnel. You never knew what you were going to see when you pulled back the door on the medevac.

The medical services were some of the best in the world, but at times Nathan's surgical skills had been challenged.

The tick-tick of the clock on the wall brought him back into focus. A little shiver ran down his spine.

A warm hand touched his arm and he jolted. 'Nathan? Are you okay?'

A frown creased her brow. The concerned expression on her face made him angry. How dare she feel sorry for him?

He snatched his arm away. 'Of course I'm fine.' He crossed his arms over his chest and walked around to the files again. 'I'm going to write up some notes. Make a few recommendations to the director. Why don't you go over to the beach or something?'

It was dismissive. Maybe even a little derogatory. But he just wanted her out of here. Away from him.

For a second Rachel looked hurt, then her jaw tightened and the indignant look came back in her eyes. The Rachel he'd known would have stood her ground and torn him down a few pegs.

But this Rachel was different. This Rachel had changed. She nodded, almost sarcastically. 'Sure. That's exactly what I'll do.' She picked up one of the pagers from the desk, clipping it to her waist without even acknowledging the act. She walked away without a glance. 'They better make cock-tails at that bar…'

The door closed behind her with a thud and he waited a few seconds before he collapsed back into the seat. One minute he was mad with her, the next he was being swamped with a whole host of memories.

One thing was for sure. This island wasn't big enough for the both of them.

CHAPTER THREE

RACHEL WAS FURIOUS. She couldn't wait to put some distance between her and Nathan.

She rubbed the palm of her hand against her shorts. It was almost burning. The contact with his skin, the gentle feel of the hairs on his arms underneath her hand was something she hadn't been ready for.

It was hard enough being around him again. She felt catapulted into a situation she was unprepared for. In her distant daydreams, she'd been sure that if she'd ever met Nathan again she would have been ready. Mentally. And physically.

She'd be wearing her best clothes. Something smart. Something professional. Her hair would have been washed and her make-up freshly applied. She would have practised how to casually say hello. All her responses would be easy, nonchalant. Or at least rehearsed over and over again so they would seem that way.

She would have a five-minute conversation with him, wishing him well for the future, and then walk off into the distance with a little swing of her hips.

She would be composed, controlled. He would never guess that her heart was breaking all over again. He would have no idea at all.

But most of all there would be absolutely no touching. *No touching at all.* Because, in her head, that was the thing that would always break her.

And she'd been right.

Her hand started to shake. Rubbing it against her thigh was no use. No use at all.

Her footsteps quickened on the descending path. The beach was only a matter of minutes away. A few of the crew members were already on the beach, sitting on the chairs. But the truth was she couldn't stay here for long. In an hour's time the celebrities would be split into two teams and dropped into the middle of the ocean.

Their first challenge would be to row to the island. The winning team would be rewarded with better sleeping facilities and more edible food. The others would spend a night sleeping on the jungle floor. Just the thought of it made her shudder. The rangers had already pulled a few spiders as big as her hands from the 'camp' and a few snakes she had no intention of identifying. The book that Lewis had given her on poisonous creatures had photographs of them and then notes on antidotes, treatments and antivenoms. It wasn't exactly fun bedtime reading.

She climbed up onto one of the bar stools, which gave a little wobble. It seemed to be designed for people of an Amazonian stature. She looked down to the sandy matting beneath her.

'What'll it be?' asked the guy behind the bar. He didn't look like a traditional bartender. He looked like a guy running between about five different jobs. Most of the crew seemed to be doing more than one thing.

'Remind me not to get too drunk. I don't fancy falling off this bar stool. It's a long way down.'

The bartender smiled. 'It's okay. I know a handsome doc that will be able to patch you up.'

She shook her head. 'Absolutely not.' She held out her hand. 'Rachel Johnson. The other doc. And, believe me, he's the last person who'd be patching me up.'

'Len Kennedy. You don't like Nathan? I'm surprised.' He set a glass in front of her. 'Don't tell me. Diet soda or fruit juice?'

She nodded ruefully. 'You guessed it; I'll be on duty soon. A diet cola will be fine.' She watched as he poured and tossed in some ice, a slice of orange and a couple of straws.

He watched while she took a sip. 'Nathan seems like a good guy. What's the problem?' The bartender's voice was steady with a curious edge. But it felt as if he'd just drawn a line in the sand as to where his loyalties lay. Great. She couldn't even come to the bar for a drink.

She gave her shoulders a shrug and took a sip through her straw. 'Some might say it's ancient history.'

Her eyes met the guy in front of her. He was handsome, but a little rough around the edges. A scar snaked from his wrist to his elbow, he had a closely shorn head, a few days' worth of stubble and eyes that had seen things they shouldn't. She wondered what his story was.

He gave her a knowing kind of smile. 'Then maybe that's the best place to leave it. Sometimes history should be just that—history.'

She'd been wrong. He didn't seem like a crazy crew member. He was a typical bartender. The kind that seemed to be able to read your mind and tell you exactly what you didn't want to hear.

She looked out at the perfect ocean. This place might not have the luxury facilities she'd been promised. But it was an incredibly beautiful setting. The kind of place where you should relax and chill out. The kind of place that probably had the most gorgeous sunsets in the world. She gave a sigh. 'Sometimes history is too hard to let go of.'

Len put another glass on the bar and filled it with lemonade. He held it up to hers. She hesitated, then held up her glass and chinked it against his. He smiled. 'Maybe you should look at this a new way. Maybe it was fate that you both ended up here at the same time.'

Fate. More like an interfering friend. She

arched her back, her hand instantly going to the skin there, tracing a line along her own scar. She hadn't thought for a second Nathan would be here. Her backpack had two bikinis that she'd never wear in front of him; they'd have to spend the next three weeks languishing at the bottom of her bag. She didn't want him asking any questions. She didn't want to explain her scar. It went hand in hand with her relationship with Darius. Things he didn't need to know about.

She didn't really want to consider fate. It didn't seem like her friend.

She smiled at Len. 'So what are your duties around here? I haven't had a chance to look around much yet.'

'Apparently I tend the bar, refill the drinks, supply ice and help the crew with setting up some of the tasks.' He took another sip of his drink. 'I've got experience in rock climbing. They said it would be useful for one of their tasks.'

Rachel's eyes widened. 'You might have experience rock climbing but I'm betting none of the celebrities have. How safe is it to make them do something like that?'

Len shook his head. 'I've no idea. I'm just the extra pair of hands. I'm assuming they'll have a safety briefing before they start. At least I hope they will.'

Rachel gave a sigh and looked out over the perfect blue Coral Sea. This place really could be an island paradise. She rested her head on her hands. 'What on earth have I got myself into?'

Len laughed. He raised his glass again and gave her a worldly-wise gaze. 'Probably a whole load of trouble.'

She lifted her glass again and clinked it against his. She had a sinking feeling he could be right.

CHAPTER FOUR

RACHEL WATCHED AS the celebrities rowed towards the island. At least that was what she thought they were trying to do.

'There's going to need to be some serious editing,' said the quiet voice behind her. 'This is really quite boring.'

She didn't turn. She didn't need to. She could actually feel his presence right behind her.

He was right. The journey to the island didn't seem like much of a journey. They'd been put into two boats and asked to row ashore as if they'd done it from the mainland. The truth was they were only a few hundred yards away. The boat with the sportsman Frank Cairns was already miles in front of the other. On a hot day his patience was obviously at an all-time low and he'd decided to do most of the rowing himself. His fellow celebs arrived onshore with big smiles on their faces.

The second boat arrived filled with long, grumpy faces and instant moans. 'My agent said I wouldn't have to do anything like this,' moaned Dazzle.

'Your agent lied,' muttered Pauline Wilding, the politician. 'Haven't you learned anything yet?'

The male and female TV presenters appeared, trying to placate the celebrities and keep the atmosphere light. Rachel scanned her eyes over them all. One of the older women was limping already. The trek through the forest to the campsite wouldn't help.

Darius appeared comfortable. The row didn't seem to have bothered him in the slightest. It made her feel a little easier. Everywhere she looked she could see potential problems. Scratches and bites that could become infected. Lack of proper nutrition. Contaminants from the horrible toilet the celebrities would need to use. If Darius had asked her if this was a good idea—she would have told him to run a million miles away.

If any patient who'd just finished another dose

of chemotherapy had asked if they should come here she would give a resounding no. A relaxing holiday in the Whitsunday islands on a luxury resort was one thing. Being dumped in a jungle to sleep for the next three weeks was another thing entirely.

She'd been lucky. She'd only had to take a year out of her medical career. A long, hard year involving surgery to remove her cancerous kidney; chemotherapy, radiotherapy and annual check-ups for five years.

Darius hadn't been so lucky. They'd met in the cancer centre, with her fighting renal cancer and him fighting non-Hodgkin's lymphoma. He'd relapsed twice since, each time becoming a little sicker than the last.

What the world didn't know was that Darius really hadn't been her lover. He'd been her friend. Her confidant in a place she'd just moved to without any real friends.

Nathan had no idea why she'd left. He'd just lost his parents and realised he needed to be his brother's guardian for the next two years. She hadn't mentioned any of the symptoms she'd had—the blood in her urine, the sick feeling and loss of appetite. They'd both been so busy in their first year as junior doctors that she'd barely had time to think much about her symptoms. A simple urine test dipstick on the ward had made her realise she needed to get some professional advice. But then Nathan's parents had been killed and they were both left stunned.

She'd held him while he'd sobbed and tried to arrange a joint funeral and sort out all the family finances. He'd just lost two people he loved. She'd nearly forgotten about her investigatory renal ultrasound. When her diagnosis had come she couldn't possibly tell him. She couldn't put him and Charlie through that. They needed time to recover. Time to find themselves. Charlie needed healthy people around him. Nathan needed to concentrate on getting his life back and learning how to be a parent to his brother.

Neither of them needed the uncertainty of someone with a cancer diagnosis. So she'd done the only thing that seemed right. She'd phoned her mother in Australia and made contact with the local cancer unit over there. Her notes transferred and her treatment planned, she'd bought her plane ticket and packed her case.

Australia had always been on the cards for Nathan and Rachel. They'd applied together. They'd meant to go together. But the death of Nathan's parents meant all those plans had to be shelved.

It was too risky to stay in England and be treated. Someone, somewhere, would have come across her and word would have got back to Nathan. She didn't want that. She loved him with her whole heart. He, and Charlie, had been through enough. She knew the risks of renal cell carcinoma. Not everyone survived. She couldn't take the risk of putting Nathan and Charlie through that.

And she knew Nathan better than he knew himself. At the time of his parents' death he'd tried so hard to be composed, to keep on top of things. This would have been the final push. Nathan would have stood by her—of that she had absolutely no doubt. No matter how hard she tried to push him away, he would have been by her side every step of the way.

In a way, she hadn't felt strong enough to be brave for herself and for Nathan too. She had to be selfish. She had to put herself first.

So that was what she'd done. She'd bought her ticket and gone to the ward where Nathan was working to let him know she was leaving.

It was the hardest thing she'd ever done. She'd been flippant, matter-of-fact. A job opportunity had arisen in Australia that was too good to give up. She didn't want to cause a scene so she hadn't warned him.

He'd be fine. Charlie would be fine. They'd been together too long. They both needed some space apart. She'd wished him and Charlie well for the future.

Her legs had been shaking as she'd made that final walk down the corridor, knowing that every single word that had come from her mouth had been a lie.

Horrible heartless lies that had hurt the person she loved.

No wonder Nathan couldn't bear to be around her.

No wonder at all.

* * *

Nathan was watching the celebrities crossing the swinging bridge made of rope and planks of wood suspended sixty feet above the jungle canopy. Any minute now...

Right on cue, one of them vomited over the bridge, clinging on for all she was worth. He couldn't stifle the laugh. He shouldn't really find it funny. But it was ridiculous. None of them had expressed a fear of heights.

It took nearly an hour for all nine celebrities to cross the bridge. It reminded him of the hysteria he'd witnessed as a student doctor at a school immunisation session when one teenage girl after another had a panic attack in the waiting room. The celebrities' legs seemed to have turned to jelly and even some of the guys made a meal of it.

Darius wasn't one of them. Neither was the sportsman. Both walked over the bridge as if they were crossing the street. Darius was beginning to pique Nathan's curiosity. What had Rachel seen in the guy? And why was he so stoic? He didn't seem fazed by the jungle—or the potential challenges. It was as if he had so much more to worry about.

There was a yell behind him and he spun around. A few other shouts followed and his legs moved automatically, crashing a path through the jungle towards the noise.

It only took him a few seconds to reach a scene of chaos. Some of the crew had obviously been transporting equipment and a whole pile of barrels that had previously been in a tower were spilled all over the ground.

'What's wrong? Is someone hurt?'

'It's Jack,' yelled one of the burlier men as he grabbed hold of one of the barrels and tried to move it aside. 'He's caught underneath.'

Nathan didn't hesitate. First priority—get to the patient. There was no way to see or assess how Jack was right now, so he used his muscle power to grab an end of one of the barrels to try and throw them out of the way. The weight of each of the barrels was extreme. 'What on earth is in these?' he grunted.

'Sand.'

'What? Why on earth do we have barrels filled with sand?'

The muscles in his arms were starting to burn as he kept pace with the others grabbing barrels and moving them away from the site.

'For one of the challenges,' shouted the crew guy.

There was a flash of pink near to him, then a figure shot past him and wriggled in between some of the barrels. 'Stop!' came a yell.

He moved forward, crouching down. 'Rachel, what on earth are you doing?'

He could only see the soles of her boots as she continued to wiggle forward, her slim body and hips pushing sideways through the barrels. None of the rest of the crew could have fitted.

Her voice seemed to echo quietly back to him, reverberating off the curved sides of the barrels. 'I've got him. He's unconscious. Give me a second.'

The site director appeared next to Nathan, talking incessantly in his ear. *Health and Safety...not safe...insurance...liability...*

'Shut up,' said Nathan sharply, tuning the man out.

'Rachel. How are you doing in there?'

There was a creak above him and several of the crew ran forward with their hands above their heads. 'Watch out, Doc. Some of these are going to go.'

Of course. They'd been so close they couldn't see the bigger picture. They'd been so quick to think about getting to Jack they hadn't considered the swaying semi-collapsed tower.

Rachel gave a little squeak. 'He's breathing. But he's unconscious,' she shouted. 'Definite sign of a head injury with a head lac, and a possible fractured ulna and radius.'

'Any other injuries?'

'Give me a sec. I can't see his legs but I can feel his pelvis and abdomen.' Nathan held his breath. His brain was trying to calculate how long it would take to medevac someone out of here. A few seconds later she shouted again. 'His pelvis seems intact and his abdomen is soft. But there's a few barrels right above us that look ready to come crashing down. Do you have anything we can use to keep us safe?'

Nathan started shouting to the crew. 'We need something to put over Jack and the doc. What do we have?'

A few members of the crew pointed to some piles of wood. But there was no chance of squeezing those in amongst the barrels. Nathan's brain was working frantically. Yesterday, he'd read a list of the challenges that the celebrities would do over the next few weeks. It sparked something in his brain. 'Wait a minute. What about the inflatables for the water challenge later—anyone know where those are?'

He hadn't even seen them but, from what he could remember about the challenge, they might help.

Ron's eyes lit up. 'Yes! They'll be perfect!' He turned on his heel and ran towards one of the equipment storage cabins.

Nathan's black medical bag thumped down beside him. He didn't even know who'd brought it. He just stuck his hand inside and pulled out a stethoscope. He ran forward and threw the stetho-scope inside. 'Rach, can you sound his chest?'

There was a muffled response. Ron and the others were still running around. The feeling of camaraderie struck him. When something hap-pened, all hands were on deck. He didn't know most of these people. He could count on one hand how many names he knew. But it didn't matter; everyone was working towards one purpose and that he could understand. It had been the way of his life for five years in Doctors Without Borders.

Ron stopped next to him, clearly out of breath—he'd need to remember to check him over later. 'We've got them—almost like giant sausages. They're thin enough when they're deflated to wiggle them through next to the doc.'

'How do you inflate them?' His brain was starting to see where this could go.

'With a pressure machine.'

'How quickly can they go up?'

'Within ten seconds.'

He ran his fingers through his hair. 'When that inflates will it push all those barrels outwards?' How on earth could he keep Rachel and Jack safe?

He turned to the technician next to him. His logical brain was trying to calculate how to do this. 'Put one on either side. They stay in the middle. That way, all the barrels will fall outwards.' At least he hoped and prayed they would. He glanced at the anxious face next to him. 'What do you think?'

Ron gave a small nod. 'I think you're a genius, Doc. Let's get to work, guys.'

They moved quickly, trying to get things in position.

Nathan took a deep breath and moved forward. 'Rach?'

Her voice echoed towards him. She sounded stressed. Climbing in amongst the barrels was probably starting to feel like a bad idea. 'It's harder than I thought. Chest clear and inflating on one side, but I can't get access to the other— he's lying on that side.' There was a definite waver in her voice. What he really wanted to do was crawl in beside her. But unless that space got about two foot wider there was no physical possibility of that—not without putting the already teetering pile at further risk.

He signalled to Ron. 'How soon will you be ready?'

Ron's face was red and sweating. He gestured towards the other guys. It might look like chaos around them but everyone seemed to know exactly what they were doing. They all had a purpose. 'Two minutes.'

Nathan crouched down, pushing himself as close to the entrance as he could. 'Good. Rach, listen to me. We need to get you and Jack out of there. The barrels aren't safe; they could fall at any minute. But we think we've got something that could help.'

'What is it?'

'Ron and the guys are going to manoeuvre some inflatables in beside you. They're rolled up like sausages and should squeeze through the gap. One will be in front of you and Jack, and the other behind. I'll give you a signal and we'll flick the switch to inflate them. It's quick. It only takes ten seconds, and once they inflate they should push all the surrounding barrels outwards. You need to keep your head down. Are you okay with that?'

'Is there any other option?' Her voice sounded shaky.

Nathan bit his lip. He was trying to make it sound as if this was perfectly planned when they both knew it wasn't. 'This is the quickest and safest option. You'll be out of there soon.' He switched back to doctor mode. 'How's the patient?'

He tried to shut out all the outside noise and just focus on her. How was she feeling in there? Any minute now the whole pile could come crashing down on top of her. He didn't even want to give that head space. He *couldn't* give that head space. Because it might actually make his hands shake. It didn't matter that he hadn't seen her in years. It didn't matter he had all this pent-up frustration and rage wrapped up in memories of her. This was Rachel.

He didn't want her to come to any harm. No matter what else went on in this world. He couldn't push aside his protective impulses towards her. He didn't dare to think about anything happening to her.

He'd just managed to see her for the first time in eight years. And, no matter how he felt about anything, he wasn't ready for that to be over.

Her bravado was obviously starting to crash. 'He's still unconscious. We'll be able to assess him better when we get out.'

Ron tapped him on the shoulder, standing in position with the bright yellow, tightly coiled inflatables in the crew's hands.

'Rach, hold on. Ron's ready. Get yourself in position.'

He couldn't imagine what it must be like in there with the heavy barrels stacked all around. It took a good ten minutes for Ron and the rest of the crew to slowly edge the giant sausage-like inflatables into position and connect them to the air pressure machines.

It was the first time in his life Nathan had ever cursed his muscular frame. He should be the one in there. Not her.

He spoke in a low voice. 'Are you sure the rest

of the barrels will fall outwards? None are going to land on them?'

Ron met his gaze; there was a flicker of doubt in his eyes. 'I'm as sure as you are.'

Nathan glanced towards the crew member standing with his hand on the air pressure machine. 'Get back,' he yelled to the rest of the crew members, who scattered like leaves on a blustery day.

Nathan couldn't help himself. He rushed forward as he signalled to the crew guy. 'Now, Rach,' he shouted. 'Get your head down!'

Strong arms pulled him backwards just as the switches on the machine were thrown. It was only ten seconds. But it felt like so much longer.

The giant sausages started to inflate, pushing everything around them outwards. The barrels teetering at the top started to rumble and fall, cascading like a champagne tower. Nathan couldn't breathe. It was almost as if everything was happening in slow motion.

One blue barrel after another thudded heavily to the ground, some landing on their side and rolling forwards, gathering momentum as the crew dived out of their path. From beneath the pile the thick yellow PVC was emerging, continuing to throw the blue barrels outwards as the air gathered inside.

Relief. He didn't even want to consider what might have happened. As the last barrel rolled past, Nathan sprinted towards the yellow PVC, crossing the ground quickly. He could hear the thuds behind him and knew that the rest of the crew were on his heels but it didn't stop him bounding over the thick inflatable.

Rachel was still crouched behind it; her body over the top of Jack's, protecting him from any falling debris. Her head was leaning over his, with her hands over the top of her head. The other yellow inflatable had protected them from behind, creating the shelter that Nathan had hoped it would.

Nathan landed beside her with a thud, dropping to his knees and gently touching her arms. 'Rachel? Are you okay?' He couldn't stop the concern lacing his voice.

Her arms were trembling and she lifted her

head slowly, licking her dry lips. Her eyes flicked from side to side. 'It's done?'

The wave of relief in her eyes was obvious. He had to hold back. He had to really hold back. It would be so easy just to wrap his arms around her and give her a quick hug of comfort and reassurance. But this was Rachel. This was *Rachel*.

He'd already experienced the briefest contact with her skin and he'd no intention of doing it again. No matter how relieved he was to see she was okay.

His black bag thumped down next to him again—the black bag he should have been carrying in his hand. Something shot through him. His first thought should have been for the patient but it hadn't been. His first thought had been Rachel.

She was still looking at him. Staring at him with those big brown eyes. As if she were still in shock after what had just happened.

He had to focus. One of them had to do their job.

He grabbed the stethoscope from her hands and bent over to sound Jack's chest. Now that the barrels were out of the way he could get access quite easily. It only took a few minutes to hear the air entry in each lung. He pulled a pen torch from his back pocket and checked both of Jack's pupils. Both reacted, although one was slightly sluggish. He grimaced. 'We really need to get some neuro obs started on this guy.'

His voice seemed to snap Rachel to attention. She jumped to her feet and held out her hands towards the crew members who were handing a stretcher towards them. It only took a few seconds to load Jack onto the stretcher, with plenty of willing hands to help them carry him back to the medical centre.

If this accident had happened in the city Nathan would have a full A & E department at his disposal, with a whole host of other doctors. Here, on this island there was only him and Rachel. She'd always been a good, competent doctor. He hoped that nothing had changed.

He didn't even glance behind the stretcher as he walked alongside the patient. His brain was spinning furiously, trying to remember where all the emergency equipment was in the medical centre.

Medical centre. It could barely even be called that. It had the basics, but was better designed for general consultations than emergency medicine. He'd expected to treat a few bites and stomach aches. Not a full scale head injury.

The crew members carried Jack inside and helped Nathan slide him across onto one of the trolleys. He did the basics and hooked Jack up to the cardiac monitor and BP cuff; at least they had one of those.

Rachel seemed to have gathered herself and was pulling Jack's notes from the filing cabinet. 'No significant medical history,' she shouted as Nathan pulled an oxygen mask over Jack's face and quickly inserted an IV cannula.

'Do we have any Glasgow Coma Scales?' It was unlikely. The Glasgow Coma Scale was used the world over to monitor unconscious patients. Rachel pulled open a few admin drawers and shook her head, passing him a recording sheet for pulse and BP, then taking a blank sheet of paper and making some quick scribbles.

She walked over and handed it to him as she slid the pen torch from his back pocket as though she did it every day, lifting Jack's eyelids and checking his pupils.

Nathan glanced at the paper. It was Rachel's attempt at an impromptu Glasgow Coma Scale. It had captured the basics—eye response, verbal response and motor response. Both of their heads snapped up as the monitor started alarming.

He ran his fingers down Jack's obviously broken arm. The colour of his fingertips was changing. They were beginning to look a little dusky, meaning that the blood supply was compromised. He swapped the oxygen saturation probe over to the other hand and watched as it came back up to ninety-eight per cent.

He looked up and his gaze meshed with Rachel's. He didn't even need to speak; she could see the same things he could.

'Nathan, do you have keys to the medicine fridge?' He nodded and tossed them in her direction. For a doctor who didn't routinely work in emergency medicine, she'd certainly remembered the basics. He finished his assessment of

Jack, recording all the responses while she drew up some basic pain medication.

Even though Jack wasn't awake they were going to have to straighten and splint his broken arm to try and re-establish the blood supply. No doctor could assume an unconscious patient couldn't feel pain. It didn't matter that Jack hadn't responded to the painful stimuli that Nathan had tried as part of the assessment. His breathing wasn't compromised so they had to administer some general pain relief before they started.

His arm fracture was obvious, with the bones displaced. Thankfully, they hadn't broken the skin so the risk of infection would be small.

Rachel spun the ampoule she'd just drawn into the syringe around towards Nathan so he could double-check the medicine and the dose. He gave a little nod of his head while she administered it.

He couldn't help but give a little smile as she positioned herself at Jack's shoulder. 'Do you remember how to do this?'

She shook her head. 'Of course not. Why do you think I'm in the anchor position? The responsibility for the displaced bones and blood supply is yours.'

Of course she was right. It would have been years since she'd been involved in repositioning bones. He'd done it three times in the last month.

It only took a few minutes to reposition the bones and put a splint underneath the arm. The most promising thing was the grunt that came from Jack.

'Can you patch that head wound?' he asked. 'I'm going to arrange to medevac Jack back to the mainland.'

Rachel opened the nearest cupboard and found some antiseptic to clean the wound, some paper stitches and a non-adhesive dressing. She worked quickly while he made the call. She waited until he replaced the receiver and gave him a nervous smile. 'I haven't sutured in a while so I've left it for the professionals.'

He nodded. It was good she wasn't trying to do things she wasn't confident with. She'd just been thrown in at the deep end and coped better than he'd expected. If the shoe was on the other foot and he'd found himself in the middle of a medical unit, how well would he do?

He might be able to diagnose and treat chest infections, some basic cardiac conditions and diagnose a new diabetic but would he really know how to treat any blood disorders or oncology conditions off the top of his head? Absolutely not.

Nathan picked up the phone and dialled through to the emergency number. Thank goodness he'd checked all these yesterday when he arrived. It didn't matter that Lewis had told him nothing would happen. Working for Doctors Without Borders had taught him to be prepared.

The call was answered straight away and arrangements made for the dispatch of the medevac. 'It's coming from Proserpine Airport. We're in luck; they were already there.'

Her sigh of relief was audible and he joined her back at the trolley. Jack still hadn't regained consciousness. Nathan took a few more minutes to redo the neuro obs and stimuli.

'Do you know where the medevac will land?'

He gave a nod of his head. 'Can you go outside and find Ron? We'll need some help transporting Jack down to the beach. They've probably cleared the landing spot already.'

She disappeared quickly and he sucked in a breath. This was a whole new experience for him. They'd trained together at university and spent their first year working as junior doctors in the same general hospital. But they'd never actually done a shift together. She'd done her six months medical rotation first while he'd done his surgical placement. They'd swapped over six months later.

He'd already known he wanted to specialise in surgery at that point, whereas Rachel had expressed a preference for medicine. They'd applied to the same hospital in Melbourne and been accepted to work there. But he'd been unable to take up his job and had a frantic scramble to find another in England. He'd always assumed that Rachel had just carried on without him. Now he wasn't so sure.

Ron's sweaty face appeared at the door. He'd really need to check him over at some point. ''Copter should be here in a few minutes. Once it's down, there are four guys outside to help you carry the stretcher.' His brow creased as he glanced at Jack. 'How is he?'

Nathan gave a little nod. 'We've patched him up as best we could but he's still unconscious. Hopefully, he'll wake up soon.'

Ron disappeared and ten minutes later the thwump-thwump of the helicopter could be heard overhead. A wave of familiarity swept over him. For a few seconds he was back in the sand, war all around, his stomach twisting at the thought of what throwing back the medevac door would reveal. But then Rachel rushed back in and the moment vanished. He finished another blood pressure reading and pupil check, then disconnected the monitor.

He pulled the blanket over Jack's face to protect him from the downdraught and any flying sand but it actually wasn't quite as bad as he'd expected. Helicopters didn't faze him at all. He'd spent the best part of five years travelling in them and pulling patients from them. But Rachel looked terrified.

She ducked as they approached the helicopter even though the spinning blades were high above her head. Several of the crew members did the same. The paramedic flung open the door and jumped down.

The handover only took a few seconds. 'Jack Baker, twenty-four. A few tons of sand-filled barrels landed on him. Suspected broken ulna and radius, blood supply looked compromised so it's been realigned. Unconscious since the accident. GCS six with recent response to pain. His right pupil has been sluggish. No problems with airway. Breath sounds equal and abdomen soft.' He handed over the charts he'd made, along with a prescription chart and Jack's notes. 'He's had five of diamorphine.'

The paramedic nodded as he anchored the stretcher inside and started connecting Jack to his equipment. His eyes met Nathan's. 'Our control centre will give you a call and keep you updated.'

Nathan pulled the door closed and backed off towards the trees next to the beach. The water rippled as the blades quickened and the helicopter lifted off. After a few minutes the members of the crew started to disperse, mumbling under their breath as they headed back towards the accident site. It would take hours to clean up. It would take even longer to write the report for the insurers.

Nathan started to roll up his khaki shirtsleeves. Report writing could wait. He'd rather be involved in the clean-up and get a better idea of the general set-up. Health and Safety might not be his direct responsibility but, as one of the doctors on the island, he didn't want to have to deal with something like that again.

Something caught his eye in the foliage next to the beach—a little flash of pink. It wasn't the tropical flowers that he'd spotted earlier; they'd been yellow, orange and red. This wasn't fauna. This was man-made.

Rachel was sitting on the edge of the beach, just as it merged with the dark green foliage. Her pink cotton T-shirt stood out. She hadn't even noticed him, her knees pulled up to her chest and her eyes fixed on the sky above.

He bit his lip. He couldn't leave her there like that. She wasn't used to trauma. She wasn't used to accidents. This was totally out of left field for her.

Part of him wanted to walk in the other direction. The Nathan of eight years ago wanted to leave her sitting there alone. But the Doctors Without Borders medic wouldn't let him. In his five years he'd never once left a colleague alone after a traumatic incident. He wasn't about to start now.

His legs moved before his brain started to function. They were on automatic pilot. He didn't even think. He just plopped down on the sand next to her and put his arm around her shoulders.

'Okay?'

She didn't speak, but she didn't pull away either—not like earlier. Her breathing was shaky and her shoulders gave the slightest quiver beneath his arm. He moved closer, pulling her to him and speaking quietly. 'You did good, Rach. Emergency medicine doesn't come easily to some folks. You acted as though it was second nature.'

'I just acted on instinct.' Her voice wavered.

'Did that include when you dived amongst those barrels that could have pounded you to pieces?' He still couldn't believe she'd done that. He still couldn't believe he hadn't been quick enough to stop her.

Her head sagged onto his shoulder. She stared out at the sea. 'I don't know why I did that.'

He smiled. 'Probably because you're head-strong, stubborn and don't listen to anyone around you.'

She gave a little laugh. 'I guess some things don't change at all.'

He felt himself tense a little. Part of him didn't want to offer comfort to her. Part of him didn't want to reassure and support her. He could feel his body reacting to hers. The familiarity of her underneath his arm, leaning against him as if they still fitted together—even after all this time.

His breath was caught somewhere in his throat. He wanted to tell her that everything changed. Things changed in the blink of an eye and the world you thought you had just slipped through your fingers.

But he couldn't let the words out.

He'd been down this road himself—acting on instinct in places where it could get you into trouble. But he'd been lucky. He'd always been surrounded by supportive colleagues. Doctors Without Borders was like that.

He didn't even want to touch on his natural instinct to the car backfiring in Melbourne that ended with him crouched in a ball on the street. Working in war zones did that to you. And it was hard to shake it off.

And, because of that, he took a deep breath and stayed where he was. Sometimes—even for a few minutes—a colleague just needed some support. He'd had colleagues who'd supported him. Now, it was his job to return the favour. No matter what else was going on in his head.

Right now it was just them. Just the two of them for the first time in eight years, sitting together on a beach.

He pushed everything else away. Three weeks on an island with Rachel?

There would be plenty of time for repercussions. But, for now, he would just wait.

CHAPTER FIVE

THE SHOWER WAS distinctly dodgy, spouting an uneven trickle of water. With thick hair like Rachel's, rinsing the shampoo out was a challenge. She pulled on a plain pink button-down shirt and another pair of khaki shorts and her hiking boots again. The smell of breakfast was wafting around. Ron had been right; the catering cabin was definitely the most popular place on the island.

Part of her felt bad for the celebrities who had spent their first night in camp, half of them lying on the equivalent of yoga mats on the jungle floor. If it had been her she would have stuck her head in the sleeping bag, pulled the tie at the top and not come out again until morning. But, then again, she wasn't here to entertain the audience.

Last night in the cabin had been hard enough. Knowing that across the simple sitting area and through the thin walls Nathan was lying in another bed made her skin tingle.

She'd spent years trying not to think about Nathan. Guilt always ensued when she thought about him. For the first year she'd had to concentrate on her own treatment and recovery. The support from Darius had actually helped; he'd been a welcome distraction. He liked to be the centre of attention in his own little world—even if he was keeping it secret. Sometimes it had felt as if Rachel was his only confidante and that could be a bit overwhelming—especially when she had her own recovery to consider.

Last night had been pretty sleepless. She tried to rationalise. She was on the Whitsundays—beautiful islands in the Coral Sea with a whole host of wildlife around her. The nightlife sounds were always going to be a little different. But that wasn't what had kept her awake.

If she closed her eyes really tightly she could almost imagine that she could hear Nathan breathing in the other room. It brought back a whole host of memories she just wasn't ready for. Her hand on his skin, watching the rise and fall of his chest and feeling the murmur of his heart beneath her palm. The soft noises he made while he slept. The fact that in their five years together, he'd never ever turned his back when they'd slept together. His arms had always been around her.

The feelings of comfort and security swept over her—things she'd missed beyond measure these last few years. And that didn't even begin to touch on the passion. The warmth. The love.

Getting up and heading for the shower to try and scrub off the feeling of his arm around her shoulders had been all she could do. Nothing could change what had happened between them. Nothing could change the look in his eyes when he'd first seen her.

She'd felt the buzz yesterday. She'd heard the concern in his voice when she dived in amongst those barrels. She still wasn't quite sure why she'd done that. It seemed like a good idea at the time—she was the only person small enough to get through the gap and to the patient.

But once she'd been in there she was scared. Hearing Nathan's voice was not only reassuring but it also bathed her in comfort, knowing that he was concerned about her. She shouldn't read anything into it. She shouldn't. She knew him. Or at least she used to know him. Nathan would have been concerned for any colleague.

Had five years working for Doctors Without Borders changed him? Had her walking away from him changed him? She hoped not. She hoped his good heart was still there. Even if he only showed it to her in a moment of crisis.

She followed the smell of eggs and bacon. Most of the crew were already eating at the variety of tables. Nathan was in the corner, having a heated discussion with one of the directors.

Rachel filled her plate with toast, bacon, eggs and coffee, then walked over, putting her tray on the table. 'Anything I should know about, guys?'

The angry words instantly dissipated as both sets of eyes looked at her in surprise. The hidden similarities between a television crew and a hospital was amazing. Rachel had spent too many years working amongst people with big egos to be thrown by anything she came across.

'Is this a medical matter or a technical matter?' she asked as she sat down and spread butter on her toast.

Nathan blinked. He still seemed surprised at her frankness. 'It's a mixture of both. Bill just presented me with a revised list of the challenges. I think some of the changes could impact on the health and safety of the contestants. He's telling me that's not our concern.'

'Really?' Rachel raised her eyebrows and bit into her toast. She chewed for a few seconds while she regarded Bill carefully. On this island, he obviously thought his word was law. To the rest of the production crew it probably was. But he hadn't met Rachel or Nathan before. No matter how at odds they were with each other, he was about to find out just how formidable they could be as a combined force.

She gave Bill her best stare. 'So, just out of interest, what would the insurance company say if both your doctors bailed?'

A slow smile started to spread over Nathan's face. He knew exactly what she was doing.

'What do you mean?' snapped Bill.

She shrugged and started cutting up her bacon

and eggs. 'I'm just asking a question, Bill. I'm pretty sure you can't have this production without your medical team in place. After yesterday, I think you'll find Nathan and I aren't prepared to negotiate on anything.' She popped a piece of bacon in her mouth. 'You either listen to us or you don't.'

She was so matter-of-fact about it. Probably because she wasn't prepared to negotiate. Employees, including herself, had been put at risk yesterday. They'd already identified a few celebrities who couldn't take part in certain challenges. She didn't even know the schedule for today. But, no matter how many years had passed, if Nathan knew enough to get angry about it, that was good enough for her.

Bill stood up abruptly, knocking the table and sloshing some of her coffee over the side of the cup. 'Fine. I'll change it back to the original plan.'

Nathan watched Bill as he stormed across the large cabin and slammed the door behind him. None of the crew even batted an eyelid. This obviously wasn't news to them.

Rachel mopped up her coffee with a napkin.

Now it was just the two of them her earlier bravado was vanishing. She was thinking about his arm on her shoulders last night and the way he'd just sat and held her until she'd composed herself. When she'd finally taken a deep breath and felt calm, he'd just given a little nod and stood up and strolled off into the sunset.

She'd no idea where he'd gone. But it had given her a chance to go back to the shared cabin, have a quick wash and change and hide in her room. She'd lain there for hours until she'd eventually heard the click of the door.

But she was a fool. He hadn't come to speak to her. And she should be grateful. Her initial reaction to him earlier had been pure and utter shock. She'd more or less said she couldn't work with him, which wasn't true. He'd just been the last person she'd expected to see.

Nathan's breakfast plate was empty, as was his coffee cup, and he picked them up. 'I've heard that filming last night varied from boring to very boring. I think they were trying to spice things up today at one of the challenges and I'm not sure I trust Bill not to still try. Are you happy to come along to the filming?'

She nodded as she glanced at the now congealed egg on her plate. Her appetite had definitely left her.

He stood up. 'I've also put up a notice saying we'll have a surgery every morning for an hour for the crew. Anyone with any difficulties. I take it you don't have a problem with that?'

She gulped. She was an experienced medical physician. Why did the thought of general practice fill her with fear? 'That should be fine.' No way did she want to express any concerns around Nathan. He'd already seen her wobble last night. That was already once too many.

'Good,' he said. 'We start in ten minutes.'

He walked out ahead of her as she scrambled to pick up her tray and she felt a flash of annoyance. Ratbag. This was something they actually should have sat down and discussed together. He wasn't senior to her. They were both here as doctors. She could almost bet if she were any other person he would have discussed this with her first.

A few of the crew were waiting when she arrived. Thankfully, there was nothing too difficult to diagnose. A few chesty crackles, another inhaler for someone and an emergency supply of blood pressure tablets for someone who'd misplaced their own.

An hour later, Ron arrived in a Jeep to pick up her and Nathan and take them to the first challenge on the other side of the island.

'Challenge has been changed,' were Ron's first words.

'What a surprise,' said Nathan. 'What to?'

'The underground scramble.' Ron kept driving while Rachel exchanged a glance with Nathan. The underground scramble was not a challenge she'd want to do. She searched her brain. Several of the celebrities suffered from claustrophobia and would have to be exempt from scrambling through the dark underground tunnels filled with a variety of creatures.

'What about Diamond?' she asked. 'I think there's too big a risk of infection.'

'I agree. I'll tell the producer she's ineligible.'

'Shouldn't that have been decided before the public voted?'

Ron looked over his shoulder. 'Don't worry about it. Vote's already decided that Darius will be doing the challenge. Diamond's safe.'

Nathan's eyes fixed hard on her as her stomach flipped over. A man who'd just undergone a bout of chemotherapy shouldn't be dragging himself through dirty, water-filled tunnels with a variety of biting creatures and insects. But she already knew what he'd say.

'I'll need to speak to Darius before he starts,' she murmured.

Ron laughed. 'Don't think you'll have a chance. They'll announce live on TV it's him and do the challenge immediately afterwards. You won't have time to talk.'

'But I need time. He'll get a safety briefing, won't he? I'll make time then.'

Nathan's gaze narrowed. 'What's wrong? Doesn't he like the dark? If he can't do a challenge shouldn't I know about it?'

She pushed back her retort. Nathan was right. It was already a bugbear that Darius was her ex.

The fact that his medical details hadn't been re-leased to Nathan was obviously annoying him. It wasn't her fault. It wasn't her choice.

But she was being paid to do a job. And she wouldn't be doing a good job if she didn't warn Darius of the risks to his health—whether he listened or not.

'He can do the challenge—and I'm sure he will. I just need to discuss some underlying issues with him.'

Nathan folded his arms across his chest and fixed his gaze back on the road ahead. The jungle foliage was beginning to thin as they reached the hollowed out tunnels at the other side of the island.

All of the celebrities were perched on a bench, talking to the hosts. Rachel jumped from the Jeep and made her way quickly to the entrance of the caves. 'How deep are they and what's in them?' she asked one of the nearby crew.

He guided her over to the side, where some TV screens were set up, showing the cameras with infrared filters that were positioned in the man-made tunnels. She grimaced at the sight of scampering creatures. 'Anything that bites and could break the skin?'

One of the rangers nodded. 'Just about everything.'

Rachel squeezed her eyes closed and pushed her way past the hosts, grabbing hold of Darius's arm. She was making an executive decision. This whole thing was fake anyway. She was pretty sure the only thing that was real was the viewers' votes.

'What's wrong, Rachel?' Darius's brow creased as he glanced to make sure no one could overhear them.

'I don't think you should do this challenge,' she said quickly. 'There's a strong possibility of getting cuts, bites or scrapes. Any break to the skin is a risk of infection and your immunity will already be low right now. There's no telling what the infection risks are from the unknown creatures or the dirty water.'

Darius shot her his famous soap star smile as he realised what her words meant. 'Lighten up, Rach. I've won the public vote? Fantastic.' He shook his head. 'I'm not worried about the tunnels. Why should you be?' He glanced over her shoulder. She could already tell that Nathan had closed in and was listening to their conversation. 'You can check me over for broken skin when I come out.' Darius gave her a wink and walked back to the bench with the other celebrities.

The producer hurried over to her, hissing in her ear. 'What are you doing? You'll spoil everything. This is supposed to be a surprise.'

She spun around. 'My job. That's what I'm doing. And what are you worried about—didn't you know Darius is one of the most famous soap stars in Australia? I'm sure he can act surprised.'

She stomped away back to the television screens. Darius was more concerned about his screen time and popularity than his health. It was maddening.

Nathan appeared at her side. 'Are you going to tell me what's going on?'

She gritted her teeth. 'I can't.'

He turned without another word and walked away.

After shooting her a few glares, the TV hosts smiled right on cue for their live broadcast. Darius was suitably surprised when he found out he'd been voted for the challenge. He smiled all through the televised safety briefing, then dived head first into the tunnels. Some of them were a tight fit. There was no way the sportsman could have forced his way through these tunnels. If Darius had been at his normal weight he probably wouldn't have fitted either. He must have lost a little weight during chemotherapy. In the end he completed the challenge in a few minutes and emerged wet and muddy with his rewards in his hands. There was a large gash on one leg and a few nips on the other from some baby alligators.

She waited impatiently for the filming to finish. 'In the Jeep,' she said as the cameras stopped.

Darius flinched and rubbed at the open wound. 'I think we're supposed to go back directly to camp.'

Nathan appeared at his back. 'Do what the good lady says. You won't like her when she's angry.'

There it was. That little hint to Darius that he actually knew her a whole lot better than Darius did. She could see the instant recognition on Darius's face as they eyed each other suspiciously.

It was ridiculous—like pistols at dawn. She was irritated enough already and this wasn't helping.

Ron appeared, sweating as always, and smiling. 'Back to the medical centre then, folks?'

All three climbed wordlessly into the Jeep. The journey back seemed so much longer. Ron talked merrily as if he hadn't noticed the atmosphere in the car, dropping them all at the path leading down to the medical centre.

Rachel strode ahead, flinging open the door and pulling things from cupboards. She gestured towards the examination trolley. 'Climb up there.'

She was so angry with them both right now she couldn't even look at them. Darius for being so stupid and Nathan for being so stubborn. Part of her knew that Nathan was right. Any other doctor would want to know the patient's history too.

But any other doctor wouldn't get under her skin and grate like Nathan could.

He was like a permanent itch. Part of her still felt guilty around him. Part of her felt angry. Irrational? Yes, of course. She was the one who had walked away. She had left him and Charlie and put herself first.

Even if she could turn back the clock she wouldn't change that—no matter how much it had hurt them both. Her outcome could have been so different. She was one of the lucky ones; she knew that. She'd had her treatment and reached the five-year magic survival milestone. That was good; that was positive.

But this whole place had just thrown her into turmoil. She'd distanced herself from Darius these last few years. He needed to find others to rely on. Coming here had been a mistake.

As for the sizzle in the air whenever she and Nathan were in the same room? She really couldn't have predicted it. If anyone had asked her, she would have sworn it would never exist again. But it did exist. Every time she looked at him her skin tingled. Every time he stood close enough, all the little hairs on her body stood on end, almost willing him to come into contact. She couldn't control her body's responses. And it was driving her nuts.

She washed her hands and opened the sterile dressing pack. Nathan had angled a lamp over Darius's leg, even though he hadn't touched it.

He seemed to sense it was wise to stay out of her way.

She slipped on her gloves and leaned over to get a good look at the wound. It was around four inches long and ragged, with a few tiny pieces of debris. She took a deep breath and irrigated with saline, removing the debris with tweezers. 'It's not deep enough to stitch. I'll close it with paper stitches. But it does give a route of entry for infection. Who knows what was in that mud or those tunnels? You're going to need this dressed and observed every day.'

Darius sighed. 'That seems like overkill. This place is miles away from the campsite. I don't want to have to come here every day. The rest of the celebrities will think I'm getting special treatment—either that or they'll think something is wrong.'

Nathan cleared his throat loudly. 'Actually, Darius, Rachel's right. And it isn't overkill. Since Rachel has highlighted you're susceptible to infection, I think it would be wise to put you on antibiotics. It's pretty much a given you're going to get some kind of infection in that wound.'

Rachel was surprised to hear Nathan back her so quickly. She finished cleaning the wound and applied some antiseptic cream and a dressing.

'It might be easier all round if either I or Rachel come up to the campsite every day to dress the wound. We can bring supplies with us and it should only take a few minutes. That way, it's pretty obvious why you're being seen. It's not special treatment. It's wound care.'

Darius nodded. He seemed oblivious to the fact she was mad at him. But of course the world revolved around Darius. At least his world did. What made her more curious was the way Nathan was actually giving him some leeway. She hadn't expected it. Hadn't expected it at all.

'That sounds great. Thanks for that.' He slid his legs from the examination couch while she got rid of the waste and Nathan dispensed some antibiotics. He held them out for Darius. 'You do realise I'll tell the producer you can't be eligible for tomorrow's challenge?'

'What?' He had Darius's instant attention. 'But it sounds like one of the best ones!'

'You can't go swimming and diving with a potentially infected leg. No way.'

Nathan was still holding onto the antibiotics. All credit to him. He knew exactly how to deal with Darius.

'But it'll look as if I'm using it as an excuse not to take part.'

Nathan shrugged. 'The producer and director have to abide by our recommendations. Feel free to say on camera that the docs have refused to let you take part. Feel free to let the world know you've got a potentially life-threatening infection in your leg.'

Rachel could almost see the headlines running through Darius's head. He gave a little nod. 'Thanks for this.' He took the antibiotics and a bottle of water from Nathan. 'I'll see you both tomorrow.'

He exited the medical centre and disappeared down the path to where Ron was waiting to drive him back to camp.

Rachel folded her arms and leaned against the wall. She could tell Nathan knew she was watching him. He started opening the filing cabinet and flicking through notes.

'That was very kind of you. What's going on?'

He glanced upwards. 'I have no idea what you mean.'

'Yeah, right. We both know you don't like Darius. Why are you being so obliging?'

Nathan sat down behind the desk. 'How much weight has he lost recently?'

She blinked. It wasn't the response she'd expected.

She shook her head. 'I'm not sure. He lost weight a few months ago. I just presumed he hasn't put it back on again yet. He is looking a little gaunt, but I'm sure once his time in camp has passed he'll be fine. All the celebrities lose some weight in camp.'

Nathan looked thoughtful. 'I don't care that you're not telling me his medical history. I just don't like the look of him.' His mouth curled upwards for a second. There was a definite glint in his eye. 'In more ways than one.' He looked serious again. 'I think there could be something else going on with Darius Cornell.'

She took a deep breath. She was having a professional conversation with Nathan Banks. It was just so weird. She'd been so wrapped up in Darius's history of non-Hodgkin's and keeping it confidential she hadn't really thought about anything else. Sometimes you needed someone else to help you look at the big picture.

She bit the inside of her lip and gave a little sigh of recognition. 'This way we get to keep a direct eye on him every day?'

Nathan smiled. 'You got it.'

So this was what working with Nathan Banks could be like. She'd waited over eight years to find out. She'd never really expected it to happen. Even though they'd attended the same university, they'd never actually worked on a ward together. Once they'd qualified, choosing different specialities meant that it was unlikely to ever happen. This had been totally unexpected.

She watched as he flicked through a few files. His hair was so short she had an urge to run her palm over his head and feel the little bristle beneath her skin. He must have got used to wearing it in the buzz-cut style while he was working away.

The first thing she'd noticed was the little lines around his eyes. He'd aged. But, like most men, he'd done it in a good way. He'd lost the fresh face of youth and replaced it with something much more lived in and a whole lot more worldly-wise.

Nathan had always managed to take her breath away. Before, it had been with his good nature, laughter and sex appeal. Now, it was something entirely different. The man in front of her made her suck her breath between her teeth and just hold it there. He had so much presence. His bulkier frame filled the room. But it was whatever was hidden behind his eyes that made her unable to release the breath screaming in her lungs.

It could be a whole variety of things. The loss of his parents. His time over the world for Doctors Without Borders. Did Nathan have a medical history she didn't know about? Why had he changed his career pathway? It could even be the fact that his brother had now settled down with a family before him. But she doubted that very much.

She wanted to peel back the layers. She wanted a diary of the missing years. But she wanted it all about Nathan, without revealing anything of herself.

Pathetic, really.

But she just wasn't ready to go there.

His head lifted and their gazes meshed. 'Is there anyone else you're worried about?' he asked.

Her brain scrambled. *You. Me.* She bit back the obvious replies.

'Ron,' she said quickly. 'I don't know if he just has a sweating disorder but I'd like to check him over.'

Nathan nodded. 'Me too. We'll get him in soon.'

He stood up and walked over to the door. 'I'm going to go for a run along the beach before we need to supervise the diving challenge.'

Rachel bit her lip. An empty beach and the open ocean sounded like a great idea. Somewhere to clear her head. Somewhere to get her thoughts together. But if Nathan was going to be there it was too crowded already.

She stood up. 'I'm going to go and talk to the

production crew about the diving challenge. I'll talk to you later.'

As she stepped outside the medical centre she took a few gulps of air. This island seemed to be getting smaller by the second…

CHAPTER SIX

RACHEL STRETCHED OUT on the sun lounger and wiggled her toes, the only part of her currently in the sun. The last few days had been odd. After the hiccup on the first day and Darius's minor injuries on the challenge, things had pretty much been how Lewis had promised. A few hours' work every day followed by hours and hours to kill. That would be fine if they were staying at a luxury resort, or in the middle of a city. Instead, they were on an island with a distinct lack of facilities and where the only entertainment was the Z-list celebrities. The days seemed longer than ever.

The challenges had been going well. Frank, the sportsman, had aced the diving challenge around the coral reef without managing to do himself any damage. The next challenge had been to scale a thirty-foot tree to reach a fake bird's-nest.

Billy X, the rapper, had proved surprisingly agile but Darius had obviously been annoyed that he'd not been voted for by the public.

His wound was gradually healing and the antibiotics seemed to have warded off any sign of infection. He still wasn't looking any better though and Rachel had started to wonder if they should be monitoring his weight. The celebrities had to prepare and cook their own food over a campfire and, even though there weren't excessive amounts of food, there was still enough to keep them sustained. Maybe Nathan was right— maybe there was something else to worry about?

She shifted uncomfortably on the sun lounger. If Darius's non-Hodgkin's relapsed he would be in big trouble. He had already relapsed twice. Each treatment plan had been more intense than the one before. She knew first-hand exactly what these treatment plans involved. He wouldn't be able to keep his illness a secret much longer.

She heard muffled voices up in the trees around her. The crew were gossiping again. She smiled. They were a great bunch but sometimes it was like being trapped on an island with a bunch of teenage girls.

Thankfully, no one seemed to have picked up on the tension between her and Nathan. Or, if they had, she hadn't heard anyone mention it.

Ron caught her eye as he walked slowly towards the medical centre. Rachel had asked him to come in twice in as many days and she was glad he'd finally showed up. Nathan was on duty and would check him over.

As he reached out his hand towards the door he winced. His face was bright red. He almost looked as though he could burst.

She hesitated for a few seconds. Nathan was an experienced A & E doctor. He could handle this—she knew he could. If she went in now, he might be resentful of her interference.

But the expression on Ron's face couldn't let her sit there much longer. She sat up and dug her toes into the sand for a second as she reached underneath the lounger for her sandals. She wasn't getting much of a tan anyway. She was too worried that if she took her sundress off and just wore her bikini people might ask questions about her scar.

She wasn't normally self-conscious and if Nathan hadn't been on the island she would have worn her bikini without a second thought. But suddenly she was wishing she had a schoolgirl-style swimsuit in her backpack—one that covered all parts of her back and front. It might not be stylish but would stop any awkward questions.

She shook the sand from her feet and pushed them into her sandals. Ron. That was who she needed to concentrate on now. It was time to stop fretting about the future and put her professional head back into place.

Nathan was feeling restless. The last few nights he hadn't been able to sleep. Lying in a cabin with only two thin walls separating him and Rachel was driving him crazy. Every time he heard the shower running he imagined her soaping her smooth skin under the spluttering water. He imagined the water running in rivulets down her straight spine, in long lines down to her painted pink toes.

The pink toes had been haunting him. It was practically the only part of her skin that could freely be seen. Unlike the rest of the crew on the island, Rachel had kept herself well covered up. T-shirts and long shorts coupled with socks and hiking boots were the flavour of the day. Even in the evening she wore long pants and long-sleeved T-shirts. The only part visible were her toes.

All his memories of nights with Rachel had revolved around short satin nightdresses and shoe-string straps. There certainly hadn't been a lack of skin.

And it certainly wasn't helping his male libido. His imagination was currently working overtime. He needed to find himself a distraction, a hobby. But finding something else to do on this island was proving harder than he'd thought.

He'd put a call through to Len to see what his plans were for later. Maybe a hike around the island would help him think about other things.

Nathan was just replacing his phone when the door opened. Ron walked in, panting heavily, with a strange expression on his face and his signature sweat marks on his grey T-shirt.

He really didn't look great. His face was highly coloured with beads of sweat on his brow. Nathan stood up quickly and helped him over to the examination trolley, lifting his legs up onto it and helping him to rest back.

He could hear Ron rasping for breath so he switched on the monitoring equipment, connected it and pulled an oxygen mask over Ron's face.

'How long have you been feeling unwell?'

'Just…today,' Ron wheezed.

The blood pressure cuff started to inflate. 'Ron, are you having any chest pain?'

Ron frowned. 'Not really. Well…maybe a little.'

Great. He'd suspected Ron wasn't feeling great but he hadn't responded to any of Nathan's invitations to be checked over. Right now, he had heart attack written all over him.

Nathan looked at the reading on the monitor and opened the drug cabinet, taking out an aspirin. First line treatment for an MI. Actually—the only treatment they had on this island. Not ideal. Still, it was better to be safe than sorry.

'Here, take this.' He handed Ron the tablet and a glass of water.

'Not really pain…' Ron continued. 'Just indigestion.'

'Indigestion? How often?'

Ron thumped the glass of water back down; even taking a sip had been an effort. 'Every day,' he gasped.

Nathan raised his eyebrows. 'Ever had problems with your blood pressure?'

Ron gave a nod.

'Does your indigestion come on when you're working?'

Another nod.

'Does it ever go down your arm?'

Ron's high colour started to pale. The oxygen was finally getting into his system and his heart rate was starting to steady.

'How bad is your indigestion today?'

'B…bad.'

'Feels like something is pressing on your chest?'

Nathan stood at the side of the examination trolley. He watched the monitor closely. It gave a clear tracing of Ron's heart rate. The PQRS waves were all visible. No ST elevation. 'The good news is you're not having a heart attack. The bad news is you've probably got angina—and had it for quite a while. I'm going to give you a spray under your tongue to see if that eases the tightness across your chest.'

It only took a second to administer the spray and another few minutes for it to take effect. Nathan frowned. In a way it was a relief that angina was Ron's problem but on an island this would be difficult. Uncontrolled angina could easily lead to a heart attack. Ron really needed to be reviewed by a cardiologist. Chances were, an angiogram would reveal blocked arteries that would need to be stented and cleared. He could just imagine how Ron would take the news. But keeping him here would be dangerous. They didn't have the equipment that would be needed if Ron did have a heart attack. Apart from aspirin, they didn't have any clot-busting drugs.

'Ron, I think you probably know this isn't indigestion you've been having. It looks like angina.

You need a twelve-lead ECG, a cardiac echo and an angiogram—none of which we can do here.'

Ron waved his hand. 'I can get all that when we get back to the mainland. I'll be fine until then.'

Nathan sat down next to the examination trolley. 'It's too big a risk. Tell the truth, Ron; you're having angina every time you exert yourself.' He nodded at the monitor. 'Your blood pressure is too high and you're constantly out of breath. Your heart is working too hard because the blood vessels aren't clear. You need to see a cardiologist.'

Ron shook his head. 'Forget it. I'll be fine.'

'No, you won't.' Nathan turned at the voice. Rachel was standing at the doorway, wearing her trademark pink. This time it wasn't a T-shirt and long shorts. This time it was a pink summer dress. She must have been down on the beach. His eyes went immediately to her painted toenails, visible in her flat jewelled sandals.

She walked over next to the trolley and put her hand in Ron's. He met her gaze immediately. Rachel had the people-person touch. In A & E you rarely got a chance to form any kind of a relationship with your patients. Medical physicians were different. They frequently saw their patients year on year.

'Ron, it's time to look after yourself. This really can't wait. Tell me honestly—how long have you been having these symptoms?'

Ron hesitated. His breathing had gradually improved. 'A few months.'

'Have you seen anyone about this?'

He shook his head. 'I've just kept taking my blood pressure tablets.' He gave a rueful smile. 'I did think it was indigestion.' He pulled a pack of a well-known brand of antacids from his pocket. 'I've been going through half a packet of these a day.'

Nathan could tell that Rachel was hiding a wince behind her smile. 'If your symptoms have been getting worse then it's definitely time for some investigations. We don't need to call a medevac to get you off the island, but we can arrange for you to go back by seaplane. We can arrange that for tomorrow. In the meantime I'll give you a spray and some instructions on how to use it. I don't want you going back to work. I want you to rest.'

Nathan watched carefully. For some reason Ron seemed to relate better to Rachel's instructions than his. She had a gift for talking to patients. Her tone was firm but friendly. He liked it.

His time working for Doctors Without Borders had been fraught. There had hardly been any time for conversations like this. As soon as he finished patching one patient—he was on to the next. There was barely time to think, let alone speak.

He sucked in a breath for a second. Something else had just struck him. He'd spent five years working with people, but not getting close—never staying in one place long enough to form true relationships. That thought started to chip away at his brain as he watched Rachel empathise and relate to Ron.

Rachel squeezed Ron's hand. 'Stay here for the next few hours, then I'll take you down to the canteen for dinner. We can have a further talk about things then.'

It was almost as if a giant weight had been lifted from Ron's shoulders. He sighed and rested back on the examination trolley, letting his eyes close. 'Dinner with a beautiful woman,' he muttered. 'I'd be a fool to say no.'

Rachel shot Nathan a smile—a smile that sent a little jolt all the way down his body. Maybe it was her humanity that was drawing him in. Even though he knew better, he'd spent the last few years labelling Rachel as heartless in his head. It had been easier to do that—because he'd never been able to get his head around the way she'd walked away and left him and Charlie.

He'd known her for seven years. The first few years of university they hadn't dated—just casually flirted. The five years after that, they'd been inseparable. Rachel had never seemed heartless to him. That just wasn't her. That wasn't how she worked. No one could spend five years with someone and not know them. It just wasn't possible to put on a good enough act to hide all your flaws and character traits for that long. He did know her. Or at least he *had* known her.

So why had she done something so out of character? What on earth had happened?

Their eyes locked. Chocolate-brown, framed with dark lashes, her eyes had always been one of his favourite parts of her. Her tan was deepening slightly after a few days on the island. Her dark hair was pulled up at either side of her face and tied in a rumpled kind of knot, the rest sitting on her shoulders. And the pink sundress covered everything, just giving enough of a hint of the soft curves that lay underneath. *Pretty as a picture.* Those were the words he'd always used for Rachel in his head. And no matter how angry he'd been with her—still was with her—some things were just buried too deep. The underlying frustration and resentment was still there.

No one had hurt him like Rachel had. What she'd done was unforgivable. But now he was in her company again he kept having little flashes of the good stuff. The way she tilted back her head and laughed when she was joking with some of the crew. The way she frequently reached out and touched someone when she was talking to them. The way that every now and then she drifted off, thinking about something else. All sparked waves of memories for Nathan. Memories of good times...memories of better times. Five years of shared memories.

Why had she walked away?

She wiggled her toes, the sand from the beach obviously caught between them. He dragged his eyes away from her painted toes and stood up. 'I'll stay with Ron for the next few hours. Come back and take over at dinner time.'

She gave a nod and glanced around the cabin. 'I promised Tallie I'd get her some petroleum jelly for her dry skin. She's trying to ward off an eczema flare-up. Do you know where it is?'

He looked up from Ron's notes and pushed the stool towards her. 'There's not enough storage in here. I think it's at the top of the cupboard over there.'

'Great, thanks.' She dragged the stool over to the counter and climbed on top to open the cupboards. Nathan glanced at Ron. Thankfully, his eyes were still closed and he wasn't watching Nathan fix on Rachel's bare legs and backside as she rummaged through the cupboard. The corners of his mouth turned upwards. Most of the prescribed medicines were easily accessible but the more routine things had to be packed away wherever there was space.

After a few minutes she finally found what she was looking for. 'Here it is.' She bent down and placed the container on the counter at her feet, ready to jump back down. But her rummaging had dislodged a few of the precariously stacked items in the cupboard and, as she looked back up, a few packages of bandages tumbled from the cupboard, bouncing all around her. It was pure instinct. As the items started to fall, Rachel lifted her hands, crouched down and curled into a ball.

The movement made her dress ride up, and not just a little. She was wearing a bikini under her dress—pink, of course. He'd already noticed the straps tied around her neck. But this time he got a flash of something else. The bright pink bikini bottoms covered some, but not all, parts of her. She was quick to grab at her dress and pull it back down, colour flooding into her cheeks.

She spun around as he got to his feet to come over and help. She lifted her hands quickly. 'Oops. Bit of a disaster.' She couldn't meet his gaze as she jumped down from the stool and made a grab for the wrapped bandages that had landed all around her. He bent to help, their hands brushing.

He saw her gulp as for a split second he caught her gaze. 'Just as well you've seen it all before,' she said quickly.

He didn't reply. He couldn't. He was still crouching down as she grabbed some of the bandages and set them on the counter. 'I'll let you get the rest. I'll take this to Tallie and be back in a few hours.'

She rushed towards the door, still talking nervously as she made a quick exit. Nathan still hadn't moved. He sucked in a deep breath as he reached for the last few bandages.

He couldn't be sure—he just couldn't be sure. But he'd seen more than enough battle scars in his time. He'd definitely seen something. But what it was he just couldn't fathom.

He'd seen Rachel's bare body a thousand times. He knew every contour of her body, every blemish, every mark. What he didn't know was the flash of a surgical scar just above her right hip. He'd no idea how far it went; she'd pulled her dress back down much too quickly. And it had only been the tiniest flash. Maybe he was wrong. Maybe he was reading too much into something.

He closed his eyes for a second, trying to visu- alise what he'd just seen. It wasn't ragged; it was clean. It couldn't be from an accident. It had to be deliberate. It had to be surgical.

Rachel had always been in perfect health. She still looked in perfect health today. So where on earth had the scar come from and what was it?

CHAPTER SEVEN

NATHAN SAT ON the sidelines while Rachel had dinner with Ron. It was clear she was onto the health promotion part. She was pointing at his plate and obviously talking about food choices. Next she swapped his soda for a diet one. Then she persuaded him to have some salad with his steak.

Ron wasn't eating much but the flushed colour of his cheeks had faded. Next, Rachel held his GTN spray for angina in her hands and talked him through how and when to use it.

'Earth to Planet Nathan. Are you home?'

Len was grinning at him from the other side of the table.

'What is it?'

Len gestured with his fork. 'You haven't taken your eyes off her for the last ten minutes. I keep expecting you to make an excuse to go on over there.'

'What? No way.' He speared a bit of his steak.

Len raised his eyebrows. 'I know.'

'Know what?'

'That you two have history.'

He almost dropped his fork. 'What do you mean?' He shot a quick wayward glance in her direction again. He'd love to say that Len was far too observant for his own good. But Len was one of the crew members he had a rapport with. He hoped Len would be on his side.

Rachel reached across the table and put her hand over Ron's, obviously offering some words of comfort.

Just as well he knew there was absolutely nothing in it, otherwise he was pretty sure his stomach would be twisting right now.

Len had started eating again. 'I knew it when I talked to her down at the bar. She mentioned you then.'

'She did?' All of a sudden Len had his instant attention. 'What did she say?'

Len laughed. 'Oh, nothing good. I take it you didn't leave things on the best of terms?'

Nathan started toying with his food. His gaze drifted back to Rachel. Her dark hair had fallen in waves over her shoulders and she'd put a pink wrap around her shoulders.

Rachel liked pink. She always had—at least seventy per cent of her wardrobe was pink. But what she probably didn't realise was just how good she looked in the colour; it didn't matter what the shade was. It seemed to make her lightly tanned skin glow and her dark hair and eyes shine.

He hesitated. It was obvious Len was waiting for an answer. 'We've not been on the best of terms for eight years.' The words kind of stuck in his throat. 'Before that, we were good together...' he paused '...really good.'

As he said the words out loud he realised how much they hurt. How little he understood about what had happened in his own life. Charlie was settled now. He'd grown up before his time and was married with a family. If his parents hadn't died that was pretty much where he'd expected him and Rachel to end up. Married with a family, probably here in Australia.

But he'd lost all that. He'd lost not just the woman, but also his dreams and aspirations. The life he'd been supposed to live. The career pathway he'd had all plotted out in his head without even knowing if he could be a decent surgeon. He'd barely had the chance to hold a surgical scalpel.

The resentment had flowed through his blood for years. He'd resented her for walking away and leaving him. He'd resented her for carrying on with her career. He'd resented the fact she'd had a life whilst he felt as if he'd been stuck in limbo.

His training in London hadn't fulfilled him; it hadn't captured his passion and enthusiasm and he'd wondered if he would ever get that back.

Joining Doctors Without Borders was his way out. It was his way of trying to live again. Trying to feel useful. He'd saved lives. He knew he had. And knowing that had helped in a way. He might not have been able to save his parents, but he had been able to save others. And for five years he had. In lots of different ways. He still felt a little numb. Some days that had been the only way to survive out there, to just block out certain things so you could continue to function. But the camaraderie with the other staff had been amazing. He'd felt valued—an essential part of the team. He'd worked hard to make others feel that way too and do the absolute best job that he could.

And he'd made friends—good friends that he would have for life.

But the truth was that everyone burned out over there. He had too.

And once you'd burned out it was time to leave. The bosses at Doctors Without Borders often recognised it before the staff did.

Australia had always been the aspiration. Now, it was a reality. But it wasn't working out quite how he had thought. Lewis was a good colleague. And the hospital he'd been working in was fine. But, the truth was, when he woke up in the morning his job wasn't the first thing on his mind.

He'd changed. Life had changed. And as he glanced across the canteen he wondered how life had changed for Rachel too.

Len cleared his throat, then took a drink of his

beer. He was off duty tonight. Officially, Nathan was off duty too. But even a couple of beers didn't appeal.

'Well, maybe it's time.'

Nathan frowned. 'Time to do what?'

'Time to find out if eight years' worth of bad feeling is worth it.' He winked at Nathan. 'I've got a nice bottle of chilled Barramundi behind the bar.' He nodded towards the wall that had the shooting schedule on it. 'There's nothing scheduled for tonight. Nothing will happen, apart from the celebrities fighting over whose turn it is to empty the dunny. Why don't you take a seat down at the beach with the fine lady and have a chat? I hear the sunsets around here are to die for.'

'Not a chance.' The words were out of his mouth immediately. He hadn't even given it a moment's consideration in his head.

Because it was more than a little tempting.

Len stood up. 'Well, if you change your mind I'll leave the bottle in some ice at the bar. Up to you, buddy. I'll see you tomorrow at the cliffs. Let's see how fast you can climb.'

Rachel and Ron had stood up and were clearing their trays. Len picked up his and walked over to the kitchen doors, exchanging a few words with them on the way.

Nathan stared down at his steak. The food here had been surprisingly good. He'd heard from the crew that television jobs were often judged on the catering and, if *Celebrity Island* was anything to go by, people would be fighting to get a job here. But his appetite had left him.

The seed that had planted in his brain earlier was beginning to bloom and grow. The more he was around Rachel, the more he realised just how much he'd done to try and avoid being in the same position again—the position where Rachel walking away had hurt more than any physical pain he'd experienced.

He'd spent eight years never really forming true relationships. He still had a good relationship with his brother, Charlie, and a few good friends from university. But other than that? The experience of losing his parents and Rachel so soon after seemed to have affected him more than he'd realised. Trusting someone with his heart again just seemed like a step too far. It was much easier to totally absorb himself in work and other issues. Trouble was, this island didn't have enough work to keep him fully occupied, leaving him with far too much thinking time.

He cleared his tray and murmured a few words of greeting to some of the other crew members. He didn't feel like socialising tonight, but on an island as small as this—with some parts out of bounds for filming—it could be difficult to find some space. The atmosphere in the cabin was becoming claustrophobic. And he was sure it was all him. Rachel seemed relaxed and at ease. She'd obviously got over the whole thing years ago. It wasn't giving her sleepless nights.

He kicked off his trainers and wandered down to the beach. The path was only lit with a few dull lights and the insects were buzzing furiously around him. The waves around this island were a disappointment. Nathan had counted on spending a few hours in the surf every day but it wasn't to be. As a result, he hadn't spent much time on the beach.

He saw her as soon as his feet touched the cool

sand. Saw the pink wrap around her, rippling in the night-time breeze.

Len had obviously whispered in her ear. A silver wine cooler was on the sand next to the sun lounger she was sitting on, a glass of wine already in her hand.

He should leave her in peace. She was probably trying to escape, just like he was.

Or he could join her. He could ask her about Ron. It was a pathetic excuse. Even he knew that. But from a fellow medic it was a reasonable question. He stuck his hands deep into his shorts pockets as he moved across the sand towards her.

She was silhouetted against the warm setting sun, which sent a peachy glow across her skin. The condensation was visible on her wine glass as she took a sip.

'Don't spoil this, Nathan.'

Her words almost stopped him in his tracks. He paused for a second, his toes curling against the sand. He knew exactly what she meant. But somehow he still didn't want to go there with her.

'Don't worry. Wine's not really my thing. I prefer a beer.' He missed out the obvious remark. *Remember?*

It was flippant, completely circumventing the whole issue. She didn't turn at his voice, just kept her gaze fixed on the horizon and let out a sigh.

She sipped at her wine. 'I'm tired, Nathan. I'm tired of all this.'

It seemed as if the barriers were finally down. Rachel was saying what had been on her mind since she'd first set foot in the medical cabin and caught sight of him.

If she'd said those words a few days ago his temper would have flared. How dare she be the one to be tired of the atmosphere between them when it was just as much her fault as his?

But the last few days had made his head spin. He couldn't work out how he really felt about her.

He'd felt it all. Searing jealousy when Darius had appeared. A whole host of sensations when his skin had come into contact with hers. Confusion and rage for the first few days. Flares of passion. His gaze couldn't help but linger on her when he thought she wouldn't notice. Certain glances, nuances, would make his heartbeat quicken and send his blood racing around his body. All sensations he wanted to deny, to ignore.

He hadn't expected to see Rachel again. And he certainly hadn't expected to feel like this around her. Feeling was the problem. It was interfering with everything and because they were virtually stranded on an island together, that seemed to amplify it all.

He stepped forward—it felt like crossing a line—and bumped down on the sun lounger beside her. Her barriers were down. Maybe it was time for some home truths.

She shuffled over a little to make room for him. He reached over and took the glass from her hand, taking a sip of the chilled wine and handing it back. His eyes were focused entirely on the orange setting sun. It seemed easier. Like sitting in a movie theatre together.

The sharp wine hit the back of his throat.

'I didn't expect to see you again, Rach.' He let the words hang in the air between them.

When she finally spoke she didn't sound quite so exasperated. 'I didn't expect to see you again either.'

She turned her head towards him. Her voice had changed; it wasn't so strong. There was the tiniest waver. 'I don't know how to be around you. I don't know how to act. I don't know what's normal for us any more. I don't think things can ever feel normal for us again.'

She was right. She was saying everything that was running through his head. They'd gone from normal to nothing. One day she'd been there— the next she had gone. With a fifteen-minute fraught and tearful conversation tacked on the end.

This situation was alien to them both.

After spending a couple of years at university together with flirtation and attraction, he'd finally acted on instinct and asked her out. They'd been together for five years—through finals, through placements as medical students and then out into the world together as junior doctors, and then senior house officers.

Their relationship had been good. There had been passion and mutual respect in equal measures with only the occasional cross word. She'd been his best friend. Losing her had devastated him at a time when he'd needed her most.

In a way it was a relief that she was struggling with this too. He'd always thought he'd been instantly replaced by Darius Cornell. He'd never understood how she could just walk away from their relationship without a backward glance. And it made him doubt himself—doubt his own ability to read people. He'd questioned that he'd ever known her at all.

She turned her body towards his. 'Would it help if I said sorry? I'm sorry that I left?'

'It would help if you told me why you left.' It came out without any censorship. Without any thought. After eight years, he had to say the thing that was truly on his mind. He needed an explanation. He *deserved* an explanation.

She paused, obviously searching her brain for the right words. 'I had to go.' The words were measured—deliberate. 'It was the right thing for me. It was the right thing for you. It was the right thing for Charlie.'

The mention of his brother made his temper flare. 'Don't you dare tell me that was the right thing for my brother. You weren't there. You didn't see. You *chose* to not see. In a world of madness you were the one thing to give him a sense of normality. You never even told him you were going. Have you any idea how hurt he was? He'd just lost his mum and dad. He didn't need to lose someone else who'd been a permanent fixture in his life for five years.'

A tear rolled down her cheek. She reached over and touched his arm, the cold fingers from the wine glass causing him to flinch. 'I know that. Don't you think I know that? And I'm sorry. It broke my heart; it really did. But I had to. I just had to.' She was shaking her head, oh, so slowly. As if she'd had no choice. But that was rubbish. There was always a choice.

It was words. It was just words. There was no explanation. No rational reason to explain what she'd done. But it was just the two of them sitting alone on this sun lounger on the beach in the glow of the setting sun. And she was confusing him all over again. How could she still do that after eight years?

He could see the sincerity in her eyes. He

could hear the emotion in her voice. She wasn't lying to him; she meant every word—even if she wouldn't explain them.

Frustration was simmering in his chest. All he wanted was an explanation. A reason. Something he could make sense of in his head. 'Why, Rach? Why can't you tell me now? It's been eight years. Surely whatever mattered then is in the past?'

Her lips were quivering, her fingertips still on his arm. He could feel the tension in the air between them, hanging like the fireflies above their heads. But there was more than that. There was the buzz, the electricity that still sparked between them.

All he wanted to do was reach up and catch the tear that was rolling down her cheek and wipe it away.

But she moved first. Something flitted across her eyes and she leaned forward, crossing the gap between them. Her perfume surrounded his senses, invading every part of him. He stopped breathing as her lips touched his. It was gentle, coaxing. Her fingertips moved from his arm to the side of his cheek.

His first reaction was to pull back. He'd thought about this from the first second he'd seen her. But he hadn't actually imagined it would happen. He hadn't even let his mind go that far.

But his body had other ideas. His hand tangled through her long hair, settling at the back of her head and pulling her closer to him.

He couldn't think straight. But he could kiss.

And Rachel was kissing him right back.

Her fingers brushed against his tightly shorn hair, sending tingles down his spine as the kiss intensified.

Eight long years he'd waited to do this again. Eight long years to feel her familiar lips against his. They fitted, just the way they always had. Memories of kissing Rachel swamped him.

In their student accommodation…in one of the on-call rooms in the hospital…at one of the hospital balls…and on the street one night in the pouring rain when they just couldn't wait to get home.

All of those memories raced around his head. This was too tempting. *She* was too tempting. Her hair was softer than cashmere, the skin around her neck and shoulders smoother than silk.

His hands slid down her back, feeling the contours of her spine and the curve of her hips. He paused. This was where he thought he'd glimpsed a scar. But now his brain felt as if it were playing tricks on him.

Every pore in his body wanted to move closer, to lie backwards on the sun lounger and pull her body against his. To feel the warm curves underneath her sundress press against the hard angles of his body. But the beach was too exposed. Any minute now some of the crew could appear. Anything that happened between him and Rachel was private—not for public consumption.

Then he felt it—the tear brush against his cheek. Was it the one that was already there? Or was she still crying?

He sucked in a breath. She gently pulled her lips from his, not breaking contact, leaving her forehead resting against his while she gave a few little gasps.

He had so many unanswered questions. So many things he wanted to say.

But she lifted her finger and placed it against his lips before he had a chance to speak. She gave the tiniest shake of her head. As if she was still trying to stay in the moment. Not trying to face up to the past, the present or the future.

His hand lifted and stroked her cheek. It was wet with tears. 'Rach?' he murmured.

She pulled back, her cheeks glistening. 'I'm sorry,' she whispered. 'I really am. But I just can't talk about it. I can't give us that time back. I just can't.' Her voice cracked and she stumbled to her feet, making a grab for her wrap. 'I'm sorry. This was a mistake. I need to go.'

She was off in a flash, running towards the path away from the beach and back to the cabins. Nathan didn't move. His heart was thudding against his chest. The caveman instinct in him wanted to run after her. But he could hardly get his head around what had just happened. Why had she kissed him?

He'd wanted to kiss her…but Rachel? Making the first move? It left him stunned.

Then his legs moved before he had a chance to think any more.

No. No, he wouldn't let her do this. He wouldn't let her disappear out of his life without explaining what had just happened. He pounded across the sand after her, catching up easily and grabbing her hand, spinning her around until she was back in his arms. His heart was thudding and his breathing rapid.

'No, Rach. Don't do this. This is it. This is the chance to clear the air between us. You have to tell me. Don't you think after all this time I deserve to know?'

Her face was wet with tears now. He hated that. He hated to think he had anything to do with that.

But he couldn't let this go. He just couldn't. It was time for the truth.

His voice was rich with emotion. 'Tell me.'

It was the thing that she'd always dreaded. The thing she'd never thought she would have to explain.

A thousand variations of the truth spun around in her head. Everything about it swamped her. The words she didn't want to say out loud just came to her lips. It was almost involuntary, but she'd been holding it in so long it just had to come out.

'I had renal cancer,' she whispered. Her voice could barely be heard above the quiet waves. The final rays of the sun had vanished now. The beach was in complete darkness, with only the occasional twinkling star.

Every part of Nathan's body stiffened. He turned towards her. He couldn't hide the horror written across his face. 'What? When? Why didn't you tell me? Why didn't anyone tell me?' He stiffened. It was as if something in his brain had just clicked. 'That's what the scar is on your back? You had your kidney removed?'

Her heart squeezed. It was obvious he was totally and utterly stunned.

The tears spilled down her cheeks and she nodded. 'No one knew. I didn't tell anyone.' Her voice broke.

His arms moved from her shoulders. This time he put both his hands on the tops of her arms. He shook his head. 'But why, Rachel? Why would you go through something like that alone? Why wouldn't you tell me?'

Anger flared inside her. Years of pent-up frustration at having to do what she'd thought was right. 'How could I? You and Charlie had just lost your parents. You were barely holding it together. I almost didn't go for the tests. I knew something wasn't quite right, but I'd pushed all that to one side while I'd helped you plan the funeral.'

'You ignored your symptoms because of me? Because of Charlie?' He looked horrified. He kept shaking his head. 'But when did you find out? When did you get the results?'

Her voice was shaking. 'Just before I left. I arranged to get my treatment in Australia.'

'That's why you left? That's why you left me?' He was furious now. The ire in his voice was only vaguely clouded by disbelief.

She shook his hands off her arms. 'Yes, that's why I left. Why did you think I left? Because I didn't love you any more?' She was shouting now; she couldn't help it. 'Why? Why would I do that? Do you know what the statistics are for renal cancer? Do you know how it's graded?

You think I should have stayed? I should have stayed and put you and Charlie under even more pressure, even more stress? You were broken, Nathan—you both were. Can you imagine getting through your parents' funeral and spending the next year trying to support a girlfriend who might die? What would that have done to you? What would that have done to Charlie? Why on earth would I do that to two people that I loved?'

She was almost spitting the words out now, all the years of pent-up frustration firing through her veins. All the anger. All the bitterness of being on her own and not being supported by the people that she'd loved. She'd had her mother, but their relationship had been different. She hadn't lived with her for more than seven years—since she'd gone to the UK and started university. It wasn't the same as having the people she'd grown to love beside her. It wasn't just Nathan and Charlie she'd walked away from—she'd also left her father. He'd tried to understand, he really had, but it had changed their relationship too.

Nathan stood up and paced the beach with his hands on his hips, his head constantly shaking. 'I can't believe it. I can't believe that's why you left. You didn't trust me? You didn't trust me enough to tell me about the cancer? You didn't think I would support you through it? You didn't think I could handle it?'

He was angry but she felt even angrier. If she could stamp her feet on the soft sand that was exactly what she'd be doing.

'That's just it. I *knew* you would support me through it. And I knew Charlie would too. But in a year's time you might have ended up organising another funeral. I couldn't do that to you. I couldn't put you both in that position.'

'That wasn't your choice to make!' he spat out. 'We were together. We were a partnership. I thought we meant something to each other. I loved you, Rachel.'

'And I loved you. That's why I left!'

Their faces were inches apart. He was furious at her, and she was equally furious with him. How dare he think she'd just upped and walked away without a second thought? She hadn't even realised that she'd been angry with him too.

Angry that he didn't come after her. Angry that he didn't jump on a plane to Australia to find her.

Of course she knew that hadn't been a possibility. She knew that he'd had Charlie to look after, but it still made her feel as if he hadn't loved her enough.

Not as much as she loved him.

Wow. The thought muddled around in her brain. She wasn't thinking about the past. She was thinking about the present. No matter what had happened between them, she still loved Nathan Banks. She'd never stopped. Her legs wobbled a little.

'I can't believe you didn't trust me, Rachel. I can't believe you didn't trust me enough to let me be by your side when you were sick.' The anger had left his voice. Now, it was just disbelief. It was obvious he'd been blindsided by this. He looked as if she'd torn his heart out and left it thrown on the beach.

'I've always trusted you, Nathan,' she said quietly. She couldn't look at him right now, with the tears falling down her cheeks. 'I thought I was doing what was best for both of us. If things had gone the other way we wouldn't be standing here having this conversation. You've no idea how many of the people I met at that treatment centre aren't here any more. I was lucky. I beat the odds. I just couldn't guarantee that. I didn't want you to have to bury someone else that you loved.'

He stepped forward, his finger brushing a tear from her cheek. 'I didn't need guarantees from you, Rachel. I just needed you.' His voice cracked and she shook her head.

'I'm sorry, Nathan. I'm sorry I didn't stay and help with Charlie. I'm sorry you had to change your speciality. But even if I had stayed, I couldn't have helped. I was too sick, too weak to have been of any use. There was no way I wanted to be a burden to you. You wouldn't have been able to stand the strain of working long hours, looking after Charlie and looking after me. No one would.'

'You can't say that! You don't know. You didn't give us the chance to find out.' Pure frustration was written all over his face.

She pressed her hand to her heart and closed her eyes. These were selfish words but she had to say them. There was no other way. She had to try and make him understand just a little. 'But what about me, Nathan? I had to concentrate on getting better. I had to concentrate on getting well. I couldn't afford to worry about you and Charlie too. I barely had enough energy to open my eyes in the morning let alone think about anyone else. I wouldn't have been a help. I would have been a hindrance, a drain.' She shook her head again. 'You didn't need that.'

Nathan didn't hesitate for a second. He stepped forward and gripped her arm. 'You had no right. No right to make that decision for me. You had no right to make that decision for Charlie. You were our family. You were all we had left.'

His words took the air right out of her. In every scenario she'd imagined over the last few years she'd always believed that what she'd done had been for the best. But the force of his reaction was wiping her out. She'd always felt guilty but she'd never really considered this. He'd been grief-stricken—already feeling abandoned by his family. But hearing his words now made her feel sick.

Yes, her actions had been selfish. But she'd thought she'd done it out of love. Now, she was beginning to wonder if playing the martyr had been the most selfish thing that she could have done.

Her legs wobbled underneath her and she collapsed back down onto the blanket, putting her head in her hands. Everything was going so wrong.

Minutes ago she'd been in Nathan's arms—the place she truly wanted to be. Minutes ago he'd been kissing her and now, with one sweep of his fingertips and the touch of a scar, there was just a world of recriminations. Exactly what she'd dreaded.

She'd expected Nathan to storm off and not talk to her any more. But he hadn't.

He stepped forward and took her hands in his. Pain was etched on his face. 'I'm sorry. I'm sorry you had renal cancer. I'm sorry you thought you had to go to the other side of the world alone to be treated. But you should have never done that, Rachel. You should have never walked away— no matter how well-intentioned you thought it was. This was about trust. This was about you and me. You didn't trust me enough to stay.' He dropped her hands. 'I just don't think I can get past this.'

He stepped back and she felt a wave of panic come over her. 'I did love you, Nathan. Really, I did.' Her voice dropped as she realised how painful it must be to hear those words.

He spun back around and glared at her. 'Really? Well, you replaced me as soon as you got to Australia. With Darius.' He almost spat the words at her.

It was pure frustration and she knew it. 'You decided you trusted him enough to help you through your surgery and treatment. Someone you barely even knew. So don't give me that, Rachel. Don't lie to me. I've had just about as much as I can take.'

He turned on his heel and strode across the beach, never once looking back.

She crumpled to the ground and started to sob. The night was ruined. Everything about this was wrong. She'd always been sure about her decision—so sure that she'd done the right thing.

Now, her brain was spinning. Her thoughts were jumbled. For the first time in her life she wondered if she might have been wrong.

It was pathetic. She was pathetic. But all she'd wanted to do was kiss him. So she had. No rational thought behind it. She'd acted purely on selfish instinct.

It was just too hard. It was too hard to be this close to him again and not touch him. In the past when she'd been with Nathan she'd spent most of her time in his arms. He'd completed her. He'd given her confidence when she'd doubted her abilities and strength when she'd struggled with the long hours of being a junior doctor.

She'd loved being with him. She'd loved being part of his family. Her own mother and father had split years before, her father staying in England and her mother settling in Australia. And although they loved her and she loved them, it had been a disjointed kind of upbringing.

When Nathan and Charlie's parents had died it had broken her. She'd wanted to be strong for them both. And she'd managed it right up until she'd found out about her diagnosis.

It had been the final straw.

And all of this was flooding back. For too long she'd kept it in a box—far out of reach, somewhere it couldn't affect her emotions. She couldn't concentrate on what her leaving had done to Nathan and Charlie. She'd been so focused on getting well and getting through her treatment that she hadn't allowed herself space to think about any of this. When her treatment was over, she'd focused on her career, trying to get things back on track after taking a year out.

But she'd never got over the guilt attached to leaving Nathan. She'd never got over the fact she didn't have the guts to say goodbye to Charlie; one tear from him would have been the end of her and she would never have made it onto that plane.

She was lucky. She'd had a good outcome and for that she was so grateful. But it hadn't been guaranteed. The prospect of deteriorating and forcing Nathan and Charlie to be by her side had been unthinkable.

And, even though she had a barrel-load of regrets, if she had her time over she would still get on that plane. She would still walk away to face the cancer on her own.

Except she hadn't really been on her own. She'd had her mum in Australia and then, even though it wasn't what people thought, she'd had Darius too.

It could barely be called a romance. There might have been a few kisses exchanged but it had been entirely different from the relationship she'd had with Nathan. There had never been the passion, the deep underlying attraction. It had almost been like a mutual support society. At times he had been a shoulder to cry on. And during her surgery and renal cancer treatment that was exactly what she'd needed.

Nathan hated her. It didn't matter that he'd kissed her back. Every time he looked at her she could see it in his eyes. If only she could have just five minutes when he looked at her like he'd used to. Just five minutes.

But the world was full of people with 'if only's. It was too late to be one of those. She wasn't here to re-examine her faulty love life. She'd never managed to sustain a decent relationship since the break-up with Nathan. At first she'd had no time or energy for it. No one quite seemed to live up to the man she'd left behind.

But this Nathan was different. He wasn't the same person she'd loved. She could see the changes behind his eyes. In the weathered lines on his face—textured in the eight years she hadn't known him. Who had he loved in that time?

What had she just done? If she'd thought this island was claustrophobic before, she'd just made the situation ten times worse.

She'd been so careful. After her initial exchange of words with Nathan she'd tried to be so cool about things. She understood his resentment. Nathan must hate her.

But it couldn't stop all the feelings he was reviving in her—all the memories. She'd dealt with her renal cancer the best way she felt she could. But it didn't stop her regretting her actions every time she looked at him.

Part of her was resentful too. How would life have turned out if the renal cancer hadn't happened? Would they have come to Australia together and settled here? Would they both have stuck at their chosen specialities? She already knew that Nathan had changed his plans—would that have happened if they'd still been together?

Something coiled inside her. Her life could have been so different.

His life could have been so different.

Their lives could have been so different.

CHAPTER EIGHT

NATHAN WAS PACING. He hated waiting.

The crew were all standing around watching him. Did they know about last night—or was he just being paranoid? Sometimes this island was just far too small.

Rachel. He hadn't had a chance to speak to her since last night and he wasn't quite sure what he wanted to say.

He could still feel the sensation of her lips on his. He could still feel the tremble in his body when she'd run the palm of her hand over his bristled hair. He could still remember the dampness on her cheek…

There was a murmur around him as he saw her approach. His eyes automatically went to the ground. He wanted to have a conversation with Rachel—but not like this. Not when cameras and twenty members of the crew were around them.

He gave a nod to Len, one of the safety instructors for this challenge, and stepped into his harness, pulling on his gloves and fastening his helmet.

Focus. That was what he needed to do right now. The time for conversations was later.

To say the atmosphere was awkward would be putting it mildly.

Neither of them could look at each other. Rachel hadn't emerged from her room this morning until she'd heard Nathan get up and use the shower and then the cabin front door banging shut.

When the director had told her that she and Nathan were responsible for checking out the safety of the challenge together this morning she'd thought of a hundred and one excuses.

But this was work. Rachel Johnson had her professional pride. And a stubborn streak a mile wide. Part of her felt responsible. *She'd* kissed him last night. She'd been the one to set the wheels in motion. Not Nathan.

Trust. The word was burning in her brain, and

it had done for most of the night. The look of hurt in his eyes had been gut-churning.

Up here, on the top edge of the cliff, with the sea winds swirling around her, trust was certainly an issue.

'There is absolutely no way I'm going down there.'

The director sighed. 'You both have to inspect all challenge sites. You can't do that from here.'

Nathan still hadn't made eye contact with her. It was apparent he'd already had this conversation because he was standing with a harness around him, gloves on his hands, receiving special instructions from Len, one of the crew members who would be overseeing their descent.

A boat bobbed on the water at the bottom of the cliff face. It was a *long* way down.

'I can do this myself, Rach, if you'd prefer.'

Nathan's low voice carried on the wind towards her. It sparked fury in her stomach. There was no way she was letting him think she was scared. She wouldn't give him the satisfaction.

She ignored him completely and stalked over to where Len was holding out the harness for her to step into. His safety briefing was thorough. She would be held safely in place; all she had to do was feed the line slowly through the carabiner. She clipped her helmet into place, then swapped her boots for the rock climbing shoes supplied by Len to ensure her grip on the rock face and pulled the gloves on to protect her hands. Lewis had never mentioned *this* in the hard sell of *Celebrity Island*.

It wasn't that she was particularly afraid of heights. She just didn't really want to step off a cliff edge into oblivion and dangle from a piece of rope.

From the corner of her eye she saw Nathan get himself into position and step backwards, easing his way down the cliff face like Spider-Man. Typical.

She turned and faced the cliff edge.

'Not that way,' joked Len as he turned her around so her back was facing the sea.

She gulped. She knew everything she was supposed to be doing. But leaning back, letting the rope take the strain of her weight and stepping into nowhere wasn't really appealing.

Len stood in front of her, talking steadily and smoothly, but the words all seemed to run into one. She'd stopped listening. Right now, she was concentrating on her breathing. Trying to stop the hysterical beat of her heart. How on earth would the celebrities manage this without having a whole bunch of heart attacks?

Len put both hands on her shoulders, edging her back. He stopped for a second and spoke again. She was pretty sure that she must resemble a ghost.

Everyone in the crew was looking at her. Watching to see what her next move would be. It was embarrassing. And it gave her the kick up the backside that she needed.

She leaned back, keeping her eyes firmly on Len as he nodded encouragingly. Her heart was in her mouth. As she took the step backwards it felt like stepping into mid-air. She was almost over the edge when she felt a hand on her backside. She was already midway. It was too late to stop.

There was only one person who could have their hand there.

Things were in motion now. Her rubber-soled shoes connected with the white cliff as she leaned back and let the rope take her whole weight. After a second, the hand moved. Nathan was right next to her.

'Are you sure about this?'

She glared at him. 'Oh, I've never been more sure.'

The edges of Nathan's mouth turned upwards. If she hadn't been holding onto the rope for dear life she could have cheerfully punched him.

'Do we know which celebs have been picked for the challenge?'

He nodded. 'It's Diamond Dazzle and Fox, the pop star. I guess a boys against girls kind of thing.'

Rachel groaned. 'Did they really get voted for the challenge?'

Nathan shrugged. 'Who knows?'

She took a moment to look around. The view from here across the Coral Sea was nothing short of spectacular. It would be even better if she didn't have a helmet stuck on her head. It gave her a real bird's eye view of the other islands dotted around them. In any other life, this might actually be a place where she could spend some holiday time. Provided, of course, that there was something resembling a hotel with proper beds.

Her descent was slow. Len's instructions had been spot-on and easy to follow.

She frowned. 'What happens with the celebs? Does someone come down alongside them?'

Nathan nodded. 'No way are they being left to come down on their own. Len will be with them every step of the way. One of us will have to be there too. I'm assuming you'll be okay if I do that? If there are any problems I'm right on hand to fix them. You'll be in the boat in case there are any problems at the bottom.'

It was so odd. Hanging from a cliff, having a conversation with someone you'd kissed the night before. Neither of you saying what you should be saying.

She nodded. 'Fine with me.' She didn't even care that the boat was being buffeted by the waves below them. She'd much rather be in the boat than on the cliff.

'Great.' Nathan bounced down the cliff a bit—

just bent his knees and jumped back, letting his rope out easily. Anyone would think he'd done this professionally in a past life.

Rachel wouldn't be bouncing anywhere. She eked out her rope slowly, taking tentative corresponding steps down the cliff face. Up above she could see nothing—just her rope. It was currently looking like a strand of thread. Could that really keep holding her?

Nathan, in the meantime, was driving her crazy. He'd bounced, and now he bounded. There were different coloured flags at various points on the cliff face. The celebrities were supposed to race down the cliff later and collect as many as they could. He was moving sideways and checking the little ledges they were positioned on, making sure it was easy to reach each one.

She'd only passed two. Both seemed to mock her on her careful descent. Thank goodness she wasn't doing this against the clock. She would fail miserably.

He bounced next to her and she could hear his heavy breathing. 'If you'd told me a few weeks ago I'd be abseiling down a cliff in the Whitsundays I wouldn't have believed you.'

His movement and voice distracted her, startled her. Her hands faltered as she eased the rope through, her feet coming up against the crumbling part of the cliff face. As the rocks loosened beneath her feet she lost her concentration. For a second she was falling into oblivion.

But it was only for a spilt second before the rope locked into place and she was left dangling in mid-air, scrambling to find her feet again.

She saw something out of the corner of her eye. It was Nathan. He'd moved sideways across the rock face and he was above her in an instant, leaning all the way back, holding his hand out to hers.

'Rach, take my hand!' He looked nervous.

As she dangled from the rope, things moved all around her, disorientating her and making her lose her sense of focus. The only one consistent thing she could see was Nathan's hand.

Her own gripped hard onto her harness. One foot connected roughly with the cliff, only for the rocks to crumble again. Panic was starting to grip her.

'Rachel, take my hand!' he shouted again. She could hear something in his voice. It was echoing the panicked reactions of her own body.

His hand brushed against her hair. He was trying to make a grab for her.

She was spinning now on the rope, her own body weight causing the momentum. If she didn't stop she'd be sick.

After last night, no part of her wanted to touch Nathan Banks again. Not when she knew the reaction it caused to her system. Not when she knew the havoc it caused.

Trust. The word echoed through her head. He'd accused her of not trusting him enough. At the time, she'd thought the opposite was true. She'd trusted him too much to stay. Too much—because she knew what he would give up for her.

'Rachel!' Now he sounded angry.

Her body acted instantly; it was pure instinct. She thrust out her hand.

There were a few seconds of scramble. Skin touching but not quite grabbing, then his hand closed over hers and he pulled her straight, yanking her towards his body.

It took another few seconds for her head to stop spinning. To gain some equilibrium again.

'Rach, are you okay?' He had her anchored against his hip, his warm breath hitting the side of her cheek.

The rubber soles of her shoes planted against the cliff. Now she'd straightened, the strain of her rope held her harness firmly in place. Her hands moved, going automatically to the carabiner.

Her breath was starting to come a little easier, but her heart was still thudding in her chest. She wasn't quite sure if that was due to the shock of what had just happened or the feel of Nathan's body next to hers.

She glanced down between her legs. It wasn't quite such a long way down now. For the first time, she thought she might actually make it.

'Rachel, are you okay?'

She still hadn't answered. She took a deep breath, securing her hands on the rope and moving sideways to steady herself on the rocks.

Nathan fixed her with his gaze. There was

so much they should be saying to each other right now.

But it was almost as if they were still shell-shocked from the night before. And this was hardly the time, or the place.

She nodded. 'I'm fine.' A few seconds later she added, 'Thank you.'

He hadn't moved. He just stayed next to her. His eyes were serious.

'What do you think?'

Her heart thudded again. 'About what?' The sea wind was whipping around them, her hair blowing across her face and her shirt plastered against her body.

'About the challenge?'

The challenge. Of course. Ever the professional, Nathan was thinking about the job.

He wasn't thinking about last night. At least—she didn't think so.

She sucked in her breath. 'I think it was my own fault I slipped. I lost concentration. Part of the cliff is crumbling. But I have to assume that all cliffs are like that.'

This challenge is crazy was what she wanted to

say. But she didn't want to seem weak, to seem scared. Especially not in front of Nathan.

He gave a little nod. 'Okay, then. Are you ready to continue down to the boat?'

She looked at the boat bobbing beneath them. The sea seemed quite calm. It almost seemed reachable.

She gave a nod. Nathan knees were bent and he was bouncing on his rope again, ready to make the final part of the journey. She just wished she was.

'Let's go then.'

She watched as he started down, controlling his descent with confidence. She glanced at the rope in her hands. *Slow and steady wins the race.* A distant memory of her father's voice echoed in her head.

I'm not sure I want to win any race against Nathan.

He looked up. 'Come on,' he shouted.

The harness was starting to pinch around her waist and hips. The tension on her rope was almost as much as the tension between them.

Would it ever be resolved?

* * *

'You're going to do the challenge in that?' Rachel couldn't hide the disdain in her voice. Diamond Dazzle was wearing the tiniest white sequin bikini known to man. Hanging from a cliff with cameras underneath? Definitely not family viewing.

But Diamond was too busy climbing into the harness. 'Do I have to wear this?' she whined, wincing as they fastened the clips.

Rachel sighed. 'I'm off down to the quay. I'll see you at the bottom.' But Diamond wasn't listening. She was too busy admiring her reflection in a mirror that one of the production crew had handed her. The celebrities weren't supposed to bring beauty products onto the island with them. But Diamond had a whole beauty counter—and made no secret about it.

Yesterday, she'd spent most of the day 'washing' herself in an equally tiny orange bikini. Rachel could only imagine she'd made most of the red-top front pages this morning. There really wasn't much to do in camp. She only hoped Diamond listened to the safety briefing at the top.

It took ten minutes for the boat to reach the bottom of the cliff face. From here, it looked a long way up—and a long way down.

She was glad Nathan had volunteered to stay at the top. The last thing she wanted to do was abseil again. Being in the boat was bad enough; the currents were a lot stronger than they looked out here.

One of the crew nudged her as Len appeared over the top of the cliff face. The challenges were normally filmed later in the day, but as this one was on the cliff it was essential it was completed in daylight.

Fox quickly followed. It seemed the pop star was a natural. He appeared comfortable in his holding position at the top of the cliff, gloves and helmet with camera attached in place, waiting to start.

Diamond was a whole other story. After twenty minutes Rachel picked up the radio. 'Nathan?' It crackled loudly. 'Anything I should know about?'

'Give me a sec,' was the sharp reply.

She rolled her eyes at the nearest crew member. 'I guess we wait then.'

After another few minutes, Diamond's perfectly tanned legs and barely clad bottom appeared over the edge of the cliff. 'Look away, guys,' muttered one of the crew members.

It was clear Diamond was making a meal of it. Rachel had no idea what the camera was capturing but she was sure that by tonight, she would be able to watch every second. She did have the tiniest bit of sympathy. Standing at the top of that cliff had terrified her. How was Diamond feeling?

After a few seconds Nathan's voice came over the radio. This time it was low. He let out a sigh. 'To be honest, I'm not happy.'

'What's wrong? Did she have a panic attack?'

'That's just it. She was making a fuss, but it all seemed put-on. She did complain of some abdominal pain earlier but she said that she was due her period and she always has some abdominal pain. I gave her some analgesia.'

Rachel kept her eyes on Diamond's descent. It was very stuttered. Had hers looked like this? Len was right alongside her, obviously giving her instructions and talking her down. In the meantime, Fox had waited gallantly until Diamond was in position and then taken off at a rate of knots, bouncing down the cliff face, gathering flags as he went. The other boat had already moved position ready to pick him up once he reached the water.

It happened so quickly. The tiniest flash of white. Arms waving. Legs flapping, a slight body tumbling, still inside the harness, and a helmet coming into contact with the cliff face.

Len was over to her instantly, talking into his radio. 'Diamond—talk to me. Guys, I might need some assistance. Give me a second.'

'What happened?' Nathan's voice cut across the radio.

'She lost control of the descent, her hands slipped and the autoblock came into play. She lost her foothold on the cliff.'

Rachel was looking up from the bottom, conscious of the fact Nathan couldn't see what she could. She knew exactly how Diamond felt. At least Rachel hadn't hit her head on the cliff.

'Is she conscious, Len?'

Even as she said the words she could hear

Diamond's hysterical voice coming through Len's mike. 'I'm dying out here! I feel sick. I'm dizzy. Oh, my stomach, this harness is killing me.'

Len's voice was steady. 'Diamond, stay calm. You're absolutely fine. I'm right beside you. You're quite safe. Your harness will hold you in position. Take some deep breaths.'

'I'm not fine. I'm dangling from a cliff!'

Rachel grimaced. This was going to be a nightmare.

'Len? Do you need some assistance down there?'

She could picture Nathan stepping into his harness already.

Len made a quick assessment. 'I think it would be better if you and I helped Diamond back down the cliff face to the boat.'

Within a few seconds she saw Nathan come over the edge of the cliff and descend easily to Diamond and Len's position. It was clear this challenge was over. Poor Fox. He wouldn't even get his five minutes of glory. Tonight's television would be all about Diamond.

She waited patiently while Diamond contin-ued to have a panic attack dangling in mid-air and flapping her arms and legs between Len and Nathan.

It was difficult to tell if it was all real or all fake. She hated being cynical, she really did.

After a few minutes Nathan spoke. 'There's no head injury, just a few small grazes on her legs and arms. We'll just take things slowly.'

She let out a long breath. They'd already had drama on the first day and then again with Ron. They really didn't need anything else.

The descent was slow. Rachel could hear the whole thing through the radio she had pressed against her ears. Nathan had the patience of a saint. He'd always been like that in doctor mode—calm, rational, reasonable. Even if he wasn't too sure what he was dealing with. How was he feeling about doing this twice in one day?

After a while the crew started to get restless. 'Can someone give me a hand with this?' The cameraman's arms were obviously burning under the strain of constantly trying to focus on the fig-ures on the cliff face while being buffeted around in a boat. Several of the other crew members moved to assist with a lot of general grumbling.

After a painstaking half hour, Nathan, Len and Diamond finally reached the bottom of the cliff and were assisted into the boat. Diamond glanced around her and sank to the bottom of the boat curled in a ball. For a second Rachel wondered if she'd spotted the camera behind her.

Len looked exasperated and he leaned over to release her harness.

'Don't touch me!' she screamed.

Rachel flinched and dropped to her knees. 'Let me loosen your harness.' She didn't wait for agreement, just moved swiftly and unclipped it. Len and Nathan were having a quick discussion.

If Diamond hadn't had Botox it was quite possible her face would be scrunched in a deep frown. Rachel ran her eyes over Diamond's skin. There were no abrasions or redness on her abdomen. It couldn't be the harness that was causing her problems.

She shot Nathan a glance. 'Diamond, would you like to sit up?'

Diamond groaned and clutched her arms around her stomach. 'No. I can't. This is agony.'

The boat was rocking fiercely on the waves as they made their way back to the quay. She placed a hand over Diamond's and saw her flinch. 'When we get onshore I'll take you up to the medical centre and we'll have a look at you.' Her eyes flickered over to Joe, the cameraman. 'And there will be *no* cameras.'

She wasn't quite sure if she said it for her own reassurance or for Diamond's. In any case, she wanted a chance to take a closer look.

The boat pulled in and one of the crew jumped out and ran to get a stretcher. Nathan was biting his lip. She knew he was still suspicious—wondering whether Diamond's pain was genuine or not.

She watched as he walked over and murmured in the cameraman's ear, putting his hand over the front of the camera. The guy nodded and pulled it down from his shoulder.

It only took a few minutes to get Diamond onto the stretcher and up to the medical cabin. It was probably the biggest strength of the production crew—they never hesitated to assist.

Rachel helped Diamond over onto the examination trolley and waited until everyone had left the room and Nathan had closed the door.

She switched on the angle lamp. It gave a much better view of Diamond's colour, which was distinctly pale. She quickly fastened a BP cuff around her arm and pressed the button to start the reading, then walked to the sink to wash her hands.

Nathan gave her a little nod. He was obviously happy to let her take the lead on this, which was a little strange—given that he was the emergency doctor.

She waited a few seconds for the reading. It was a little below average but not worryingly so. 'Diamond, I'm going to put my hands on your stomach. Is that okay?'

The model's eyes widened. 'Do you have to?'

She nodded. 'Nathan told me earlier today you complained of period pain. Is that normal for you?'

Diamond nodded. 'I always get it. Just cramps—

and that's what it was like this morning. But this is much worse. The painkillers haven't touched it.'

'Any other symptoms? Have you been going to the toilet frequently?'

Diamond wrinkled her nose. 'Maybe.'

'What about your bowels? Are they moving normally?'

'*Eeoow.* Don't ask about things like that.'

Rachel smiled. 'I have to. It's part of being a doctor.'

Diamond winced again. 'No problems then.'

She flinched as Rachel gently laid her hands on her stomach.

'Can you tell me where the worst of the pain is? In your front or around your back?' She pressed very gently. Diamond seemed to wince at every movement, then she pulled her knees up quickly.

'*Yaoow!* It's definitely worse on that side.'

Rachel lifted her hands. 'Have you been eating? Feeling sick, nauseous?'

'I've felt sick most of the day. But I haven't actually been sick.'

Rachel bit her lip. Diamond's pain was on the opposite side from her appendix. 'Do you think you could give me a urine sample? I'd like to dip-stick it for any sign of infection.'

Diamond groaned. 'You want me to get up?'

Rachel nodded. 'We don't exactly have a lot of equipment here. I'll help you to the bathroom. It's only a few steps.'

She gently swung Diamond's legs to the edge of the trolley and helped her limp over to the bathroom, handing her a collection bottle.

Rachel and Nathan waited outside the door. He glanced at her, mouthing the words, 'What do you think? UTI or ectopic?'

She lifted her shoulders. 'Could be either.'

After a few minutes Diamond opened the door and handed her specimen container over with shaky hands.

'Your colour's not too good. Let me help you back over.' Nathan didn't wait. He picked her up in his arms and carried her over to the trolley.

Rachel took the specimen over to the counter-top and dipsticked it with a multistick for blood and protein, and dropped some onto a preg-nancy test. It would take at least a minute until it showed.

She took a few steps nearer Diamond. 'I know that you said your period is due, but can you tell me how long it is since your last one?'

Diamond screwed up her face, her arms still across her belly. 'I'm not that regular. Probably around six weeks. I always get cramp—but not usually as bad as this. I feel as if it could come any minute.'

Nathan wound the BP cuff back around her arm. 'I'm just going to check this again.' He pressed the button. 'This will get quite tight.'

Rachel glanced over towards the tests on the bench. A positive pregnancy test and some blood in her urine. She swallowed. 'Diamond, is there any chance you could be pregnant?'

Diamond's eyes opened quickly. It was almost as if she were trying to rationalise the possibility.

Rachel reached for her hand. 'I don't think the pain you're experiencing is normal period pain. I think it's something else.'

Nathan moved closer. 'Diamond, we don't have all the facilities here that we need.' His voice was sympathetic. 'Your urine shows a positive pregnancy test, but it also had some blood in it—even though you might not have noticed. Your blood pressure is on the low side and with the pain you have in your side—it could be that you're having an ectopic pregnancy.'

Diamond looked stunned. She started shaking her head. 'I can't be pregnant. I can't be.'

Rachel squeezed her hand. 'Have you had un-protected sex in the last six weeks?'

Her pale cheeks flushed. 'Well….yes.'

'Have you had any bleeding at all?'

She glanced between Rachel and Nathan. 'I had a tiny bit of spotting yesterday. I just thought my period was starting.'

Nathan nodded. 'Do you know much about ectopic pregnancy, Diamond?'

She shook her head quickly. 'Nothing.' There was something about Diamond's wide-eyed reaction that made him slow down.

He glanced towards Rachel. He was surprising her—which was ridiculous, as Nathan had always been a compassionate doctor. The truth was they'd both had doubts about Diamond's symptoms.

He spoke slowly. It was obvious he was trying to make things as clear as possible, whilst he knew he was dealing with a highly sensitive issue.

'In an ectopic pregnancy the embryo doesn't implant and grow in the womb as it should. It gets stuck somewhere along the fallopian tube and the embryo starts to grow there. That would be why you're having pain. There isn't room for the embryo to grow.'

She looked scared. 'So what happens now?'

He spoke carefully. 'In an ideal world, we'd do an ultrasound to confirm our diagnosis. But we don't have ultrasound equipment here, so we just need to go on your symptoms and the fact you've had a positive pregnancy test. We class this as an emergency. Your fallopian tube can rupture and cause internal bleeding. Because of that, we'll arrange a medevac to take you off the island and to a hospital on the mainland where it's likely you'll need to go for surgery.'

'I need to leave the show?'

It wasn't the response Rachel was expecting to hear. But Diamond just looked stunned.

'You definitely need to leave the show.'

She nodded. 'Okay. Can someone phone my agent?'

Rachel and Nathan exchanged glances. Diamond seemed to have switched into professional mode.

Rachel walked over and took her hand. 'No problem. Nathan will get someone to do that.' He gave a quick nod. Rachel walked over to the medicine cabinet and quickly drew up some analgesia. 'I'm going to give you something for the pain meantime'

Rachel leaned forward and kept talking as she administered the injection, 'This is an emergency, Diamond. I don't want to scare you, but if your fallopian tube ruptures it will cause more pain and the bleeding can be serious. You need to be in a place that can deal with that kind of emergency.' She held out her hands and looked around. 'And that's certainly not here.'

Nathan nodded in agreement. 'We don't have any medication that we can give you here to try and stop the embryo growing. You have to go to a specialist hospital.'

Diamond winced as she tried to sit up. Her

eyes widened and she fixed them on Rachel. 'I'm pregnant? I'm really pregnant?' The look of disbelief on her face was obvious. It seemed things were just starting to sink in.

Rachel walked back over to Diamond and started the BP monitor again. Diamond looked completely shocked.

'I'm pregnant?' she asked again.

Rachel chose her words carefully. If a pregnancy was ectopic there was no hope for the growing embryo. Diamond's reactions earlier had been odd—almost as if she wasn't taking in what they'd been saying to her. Maybe the truth was just hitting her now.

Nathan appeared at the other side of the trolley. It was as if he sensed how she might react.

Something squeezed inside Rachel. This was a horrible experience for any woman. She'd never been in this position. Chances were, after the treatment she'd received for her renal cancer, she might never be in the position to be pregnant.

Although they'd been junior doctors, she and Nathan had never been afraid to talk about the future. They'd been so sure that their future would be together. They'd talked about eventually getting married and having children together, Nathan as a surgeon and Rachel probably working as a GP at that point. Looking back, it had been a strange conversation for two young, ambitious, career-orientated people to have. But both had loved the idea of having a family together. As doctors, they both knew they would need support with their children. Nathan had been adamant that he, as well as Rachel, should only work four days a week. That way, both would have a day at home with the kids, with Nathan's parents or Rachel's dad helping on the other days.

She flinched. More hopes and dreams that had disappeared in the blink of an eye. Destroyed by a car crash and a cancer diagnosis.

Had she really taken on board how big an impact these things had had on both their lives?

She lifted her head. Nathan's gaze interlocked with hers, his green eyes holding her steady. She swallowed. There was pain etched on his face. It was almost as if all the same thoughts were going through his head. Did he remember the conversations they used to have about family?

Rachel took a deep breath and turned her attention back to her patient. 'You had a positive pregnancy test and the symptoms you're showing suggest you have an ectopic pregnancy. Nathan explained earlier that the embryo is growing in your fallopian tube instead of in your womb. That's why you're in so much pain.' She squeezed Diamond's hand. 'I'm really sorry, Diamond. But what this means is that this pregnancy isn't viable. This pregnancy could never result in a baby for you.'

She hated saying those words out loud because she already knew the impact it would have on their patient.

Diamond shook her head as a tear slid down her cheek. 'But I always thought I couldn't get pregnant.'

'Why did you think that?' Nathan's voice cut in before Rachel had a chance to reply.

'They told me my tubes were scarred. They told me if I ever wanted to get pregnant I'd probably need to use IVF.' She was shaking her head in disbelief.

Scarred tubes—exactly the kind of place an

embryo could implant. It made the diagnosis of ectopic pregnancy even more likely.

Nathan checked her BP reading. Low, but steady. 'You saw an ob-gyn?'

Diamond's face flushed a little. 'I had an infection a few years ago. She did some follow-up tests.'

He'd read her medical notes; this hadn't been in them. She clearly wanted to keep it secret.

He nodded sympathetically. 'It makes the chances of this being an ectopic pregnancy even more likely, but we can't tell you for sure. They'll need to scan you once you reach the mainland. How is your pain? Is it any better since Rachel gave you the injection?'

Diamond gave a little nod just as there was a knock at the door. 'Five minutes, docs,' came the shout.

Rachel still wasn't entirely sure about Diamond. 'How do you feel about transferring in the medevac?'

There was no getting away from it. The medevac could be terrifying. The noise and buffeting from the air currents could make it a bumpy trip. Rachel wasn't certain that she'd like to be the one going.

Diamond nodded slowly. 'I really can't come back?' Her voice was quiet, almost whispered.

'Absolutely not.' Nathan didn't hesitate. 'You need to be in a place where you can be taken care of and get the support that you need. The island isn't the place for that.'

Her eyes were downcast and Rachel wondered if the true nature of what had happened was now sinking in. 'Is there someone you'd like me to phone for you?' She wasn't sure if Diamond had a partner or a boyfriend. She didn't really keep track of celebrity relationships. Being in the spotlight herself for a few months had been bad enough. Whether the pregnancy had been planned or not, losing a baby could be a big shock to any couple.

Diamond shook her head. The tears were flowing freely now. 'I think that's a phone call I need to make myself.' Her voice was shaking now and Rachel could feel tears springing to her own eyes.

Nathan walked over and put his arm around Diamond's shoulders. 'I'm really sorry, Diamond.

I'm really sorry about your baby and I'm really sorry it happened here.' He glanced at Rachel. 'We're going to give you something else for the flight. It can be a little bumpy and I want to make sure your pain is under control and you're as relaxed as possible.'

He walked over and unlocked the medicine cupboard, taking out another vial and turning it for Rachel to double-check. She nodded as she dialled the number and spoke urgently into the phone, giving the medevac all the details they would need.

Nathan administered the medicine quickly.

Rachel nodded as she left the cabin. 'I'll get the crew to prepare for the medevac and I'll let the producer know what is happening.'

Thank goodness they were out of earshot because Phil, one of the producers, nearly blew a gasket when she told him she'd arranged a medevac for Diamond.

'What? You've got to be joking. We need her for the viewing figures. This will affect our ratings.'

'And if she doesn't get appropriate treatment

this could affect her life,' she said sharply. She was getting tired of this—tired of how some people didn't seem to care about the actual individuals—just the figures.

In fact, she was getting tired of everything. Tired of being trapped on an island with Nathan. Tired of the way they tiptoed around each other constantly. Tired of her conflicting emotions around him. And the fact that on an island like this there was no privacy, no escape.

Next time she saw Lewis Blake she was going to kill him with her bare hands. It didn't matter what the salary was here—he'd got more than his money's worth.

By the time she'd finished with Phil, she received a message to say the medevac had arrived. The crew, as always, were only too happy to assist.

As they headed down to the beach the downdraught from the helicopter swooshed around them and Diamond started to shake. Nathan kept his arm around her the whole time. It only took five minutes to do the handover and get her loaded on board. The paramedic winked at them both. It was the same guy who'd picked up Jack. 'This is getting to be a habit. Here's hoping I don't hear from you two again.'

Nathan pulled the door closed and retreated to the trees, watching the helicopter take off before heading back to the cabin. They could hear Phil somewhere in the complex, shouting at the top of his voice.

Nathan gave Rachel an ironic smile. 'So much for working twelve hours in three weeks.'

Her eyebrows lifted. 'Lewis used that line on you too?'

'Oh, yes.'

Their smiles locked for a few seconds. She felt the buzz. It was hanging in the air between them. Familiar. Sparking lots of warm, passionate memories.

Something washed over her. More than regret. More than sadness. The awareness of what might have been. The loss of the life they could have had together.

She couldn't help it. It brought instant tears to her eyes. Nathan had been her soulmate, the person she'd thought she would grow old with.

And in two fell swoops everything had changed.

A driver's momentary distraction on a country road, and the view of cancer cells under the microscope.

Where would they have been in the life they should have lived? Married? Probably. With children? She certainly hoped so. It didn't matter that this parallel universe didn't exist. It didn't matter that this was all a figment of her imagination.

At times, during her treatment, it had been the only thing that had kept her going. Imagining that Nathan had built a new life for himself, met someone else and moved on had been just too much for her. It didn't matter that she'd told herself that was what she wanted for him. A long lifetime of happiness.

Her own heart told her differently.

'Rachel?' His voice was quiet and he stepped closer to her. 'Are you okay?'

He must have noticed the tears glistening in her eyes. It would be so easy to make an excuse—to say it was the sand thrown up by the helicopter blades, to say it was the sea breeze in her eyes. But she didn't want to. She didn't want to tell lies. She was so tired of it all. Keeping her guard up continually around Nathan was wearing her down.

She fixed on his neon green eyes. She'd always loved looking into Nathan's eyes. She'd spent the last week virtually avoiding them, skirting past them whenever she could for fear of the memories they might stir up.

'No,' was all she replied.

He blinked and waited a few seconds, his gaze never wavering from hers. 'Me neither.' His words were low. So low she wondered if she'd even heard them.

He reached over and touched her arm. She froze, her breath stuck in her throat.

'Rachel, do you want to have dinner tonight—just you and me?'

She nodded.

He didn't smile. 'We both have a few things to do. And we can't talk in the canteen. I'll meet you back here at seven and arrange some food for us.'

The filming for the day was already done. By seven the sun would almost be setting and the beach should be quieter.

'Sounds fine. I'll see you then.' She turned and walked away, her heart thudding in her chest.

Dinner.

It sounded so simple. But it wouldn't just be dinner. They both knew that. It would be so much more. It was time to put the past to rest.

CHAPTER NINE

NATHAN LOOKED DOWN at the hamper one of the chefs had given him. It should be perfect. It was packed with all the kind of foods that he enjoyed—and the ones that he remembered Rachel liked.

Stuffed in next to the food were two bottles of wine and a couple of glasses nabbed from behind the bar.

Would he even be able to eat anything? His stomach turned over. There was no doubt the attraction between him and Rachel was still there. The attraction had never been in doubt. It was the history that was the problem.

He couldn't act on his instincts around her. Every time he looked at her he felt his self-protection barriers fall into place. Guys didn't admit to being hurt. Guys didn't admit to being broken-hearted.

But he'd felt both when Rachel had left.

Eight years on, he hadn't moved past that and it was crippling him. He hadn't really formed a proper relationship since then. Initially he'd been too busy watching out for Charlie, then he'd been too busy working.

For the last five years he'd been trying to save the world. He hadn't been able to save his parents—they'd been left trapped in their twisted car for the best part of an hour before anyone had found them. By then, both of them had been unconscious. His mother had never made it to the hospital. His father had barely survived the journey and had died before Nathan was notified about the accident. At least with Doctors Without Borders he knew his work counted. He knew he could look back on the lives he'd saved—the difference he'd made. And in a tiny way it had helped patch his heart back together.

But recognition was dawning slowly—he'd spent so much time trying to save other people and not enough time trying to save himself.

Seeing Rachel had brought everything to the forefront again. There were things—feelings—

that he couldn't deny. At some point in his life he was going to have to move on. He'd just never expected that moving on with Rachel might even be a remote possibility. He still wasn't entirely sure it was. But tonight it was time to find out.

All he felt right this minute was hideous guilt. Rachel had told him she'd had renal cancer. And, instead of asking her all the questions he should have, he'd been so overcome with anger that he'd forgotten all the important stuff. He'd forgotten to ask her all the medical questions that had been spinning around in his brain ever since. Her treatment—and the outcome. The future. What kind of guy was he? What kind of friend was he?

He hated this. He hated all of this.

He walked down to the beach. There were a few people around, chatting and talking at the bar.

He didn't want to join in. He was already too wound up. Chances were, they'd meet and be fighting within five minutes. But fighting wasn't what he wanted to do with Rachel.

His fingers were itching to touch her. He wanted to run them through her shiny hair; he wanted to stroke them across her perfect skin. He wanted to touch the place where she had that scar. He wanted to kiss it.

He wanted to let her know that the renal cancer didn't change how he felt about her. Wouldn't *ever* change how he felt about her. More than anything, he wanted her lips to surrender to his. It was bad enough his dreams at night were haunted by her. He'd started to daydream about her too.

He couldn't go on like this. He couldn't function. Things just had to come to a head. Who knew where it would lead?

But the electricity in the air between them could light up this whole island. It was time to find out if she agreed.

Rachel stared in the mirror. She'd showered and her hair was washed and dried. She'd put on some bronzer, mascara and lipstick. She should be ready. She *could* be ready. If only she could decide what to wear.

Maybe it was delaying tactics. Maybe it was because her stomach was churning and she wondered if the nerves could make her sick. Or maybe it was because, deep down, she wanted to look perfect for Nathan.

Her rucksack was upended on the bed. Three pink sundresses, four pink shirts and three T-shirts all seemed to mock her. Nothing was right. Nothing *felt* right. And she wasn't sure why it was so important.

She rummaged around the bottom of the rucksack to see if she'd missed anything. Her hand slithered over some material and she pulled it out. A pink sequin bikini. She'd thrown it back inside as soon as she'd realised Nathan was here—her scar would have raised too many questions she didn't want to answer.

But now Nathan knew. Now, there was nothing to hide.

Except how he felt about what she'd done. Except the whole reality of her non-relationship with Darius. It was time to come clean about that. It was time to clear the air between them. Could that even be done?

Her stomach twisted. She was going to a beach.

The night air was still warm. There were lots of reasons why her bikini was the perfect outfit.

Her black sheer kaftan with silver embroidery was hanging on the other side of the room. She walked over and grabbed it.

More than anything, she wanted Nathan to stop looking at her the way he did. With recriminations. With an undercurrent of anger. She wanted Nathan to look at her the way he'd used to. With love. With passion—even devotion. Just the way she'd looked at him too.

She'd almost seen it the other night before she'd ruined everything by telling him about the renal cancer. Maybe that was all he wanted to do tonight—ask her more questions about the cancer. Maybe she was getting herself all worked up over an attraction that wasn't even there.

She glanced at her watch—it was after seven. Nathan would be wondering where she was. She pulled on the bikini and kaftan before she changed her mind and slipped her feet into some sandals. There was no need for anything else. There was no time to think about anything else.

Her initial quick steps slowed as she reached

the beach. She was nervous. After eight years, the thought of spending time alone with Nathan made her stomach flip over. In good ways and in bad.

Part of her couldn't wait for this to start and part of her couldn't wait for this to be over. She wanted to be with Nathan. She wanted to spend time in his company. She wanted to get past the bitterness, past the recriminations. She wanted to find out how Nathan really was. How he'd spent the last eight years and, most importantly, if anyone had touched his heart. She wanted to acknowledge the buzz between them, the attraction. She wanted to know if she could trust her instincts and that, no matter what had happened between them, he wanted to act on them as much as she did.

Nothing in her head was certain right now.

She walked down the path. To her right, several members of the crew were at the bar, laughing and joking together. To her left were the sun loungers. All were empty except one. Nathan was sitting staring at the ocean with a basket at his feet.

The corners of his lips turned upwards as she walked towards him. He was so handsome when he smiled. It made her skin tingle and her heart melt—it was a pity he didn't do it more often. He didn't even hide the fact he was looking at her bare legs. He was dressed casually too, in shorts and a T-shirt. If he was surprised at her lack of clothes he didn't mention it. He just continued with the appreciative looks. It made her whole body shiver with anticipation.

He stood up as she approached and lifted the basket. Her stomach flip-flopped. She was even more nervous than she'd expected.

He gave a little nod. 'Let's get away from everyone. There's another beach just around the corner, set in a cove of its own.'

Let's get away from everyone. He had no idea what those words were doing to her heart rate and her adrenalin levels.

'Really? I had no idea.' She was trying so hard to appear casual but her smile had spread from ear to ear. Why hide it?

He grinned and raised his eyebrows. 'Neither did I. Len told me when he caught me raiding the bar.' He picked up a blanket from the lounger and took a few steps down the beach.

'What did you get from the bar?'

'Some wine. Rosé.' His footsteps hesitated. 'It's still your favourite, isn't it?'

Even her insides were smiling now. He'd remembered. He'd remembered her favourite drink.

'Yes. It's still my favourite,' she said quietly.

'Good.'

There was a gentle breeze as they walked along the beach together. The orange sunset reflected across the undulating waves and the muted burnished rays across the water gave a remarkable sense of calm. As they walked, behind them, in amongst the trees, the insect life was rustling and chirping.

But the beach was quiet, the only noise the rippling waves on the sand.

As the voices behind them drifted further and further away Rachel felt herself relax a little. The lights from the bar area faded and as they rounded the bay towards the other beach the only light was the orange setting sun.

Nathan shook out the blanket and set it down on

the sand. She hesitated as he opened the basket and took out the wine and some glasses. 'Aren't you going to sit?' he asked as he unscrewed the bottle.

How close should she sit? The blanket wasn't too big and as she lowered herself down her bare legs brushed against his.

It was like an electric jolt and his head lifted sharply, their gazes meshing. He handed her a glass without saying a word. Something fired inside her. All of a sudden this felt immediate. She didn't want to wait. She didn't want to think about this any longer. Words could get in the way of what she really wanted to do. She glanced over her shoulder. They were definitely alone and undisturbed.

When she reached for the glass she was slow, deliberate. Her fingers brushed over his.

His gaze was fixed on hers. It was almost as if he couldn't tear it away. Almost as if this was the moment they had been waiting for.

'How are you, Rachel?' he asked. She felt as if something had blown away in the gentle breeze. It was almost as if they hadn't seen each other before this. There was no guilt or recrimination. This was a new start.

It was time for complete honesty. 'Pretty rubbish,' she whispered.

This was it. This was where the doors were finally opened. This was the point of no return.

Nathan reached his hand over and touched hers. She didn't flinch. She didn't pull it away. 'Let me start,' he said slowly. 'I have to apologise.'

'What for?'

He took a deep breath. 'I didn't even ask you.' He fixed his eyes on the horizon. He couldn't even look at her right now. He was still angry with himself for not asking the questions he should have.

'Ask me what?'

He ran his hand over his short hair. 'What stage cancer you had—what treatment you had. You never even told me how you discovered it.' He shook his head. 'I should have asked—I'm sorry. When you told me that night I was shocked. I just needed a bit of space to get my head around it.'

She bit her lip. He could tell she didn't really know where to start.

'I was tired.' It seemed the simplest explanation and, as a medic, he knew it was probably the truest. 'My symptoms were mild. Fatigue, a bit of weight loss, just generally feeling unwell. I couldn't sleep very well—and that was even before your parents' accident. So I couldn't put it down to that. I had a few unexplained temperatures. Then, one day, I dipsticked my urine in the ward. Once I realised I had blood in it and not a simple infection I started to piece everything together.' She shook her head. 'I didn't like what I found. But my appointment for investigation came just a few weeks after the funeral. We'd had too much else to deal with—too much else to think about and I almost never went.'

His stomach turned over. Was he ready for this? Was he ready to hear that she'd been so worried about him she hadn't been thinking about herself? 'What stage were you at?'

She took a sip of wine. 'I had stage three. The tumour was bigger than seven centimetres and had spread through the outer covering of the kidney to the adrenal gland. I needed a total nephrec-tomy and some radiotherapy and chemotherapy.'

He nodded his head slowly while his insides cringed, twisting and turning at the thought of cancer invading the body of someone he loved. He knew exactly how serious her cancer had been and how invasive the treatment would have been. Every doctor knew about the staging of cancers.

He put his head in his hands. What if she'd ig-nored it? What if she'd been so busy with him and Charlie that her renal cancer had got even worse? The thought made him feel sick to his stomach.

He waited a few seconds then spoke, his voice steady. 'Would you have told me? If my parents hadn't died—would you have told me then?'

He heard her suck in a breath. She took a few seconds to answer the question. 'Of course I would, Nathan.'

He squeezed his eyes shut. He was trying not to be frustrated but the truth was he wanted to scream and shout. He shook his head. After a few seconds some strangulated words came from his throat. 'Everything—everything changed.

When my parents died, everything I'd planned just changed in an instant.'

He turned to face her, still shaking his head. He couldn't contain anything that was inside any more. Eight years' worth of grief and frustration came bubbling to the surface. 'You. You left. You wouldn't have if my parents had been alive. You would have told me you were ill. I could have supported you. If they'd still been there I wouldn't have changed my speciality—I wouldn't have needed to; Charlie would have been fine. I could still have been a surgeon.' His fists were clenched and his jaw tight. 'I mean, what's the point?' It was as if now the words had started he just couldn't stop. 'What's the point of being a doctor if you can't save the people that you love? One second—one second on one road on one night—changed everything about my life. I lost you. I lost my career. I lost them.'

He'd never felt so angry. Eight years ago he'd never been prone to temper flares or angry outbursts. Even when his parents had died he'd been quiet, obviously upset, but subdued. She shrank back a little.

He stood up and started pacing. 'They were trapped in their car for an hour. If they'd had medical assistance they might have lived. Where were we that night? We were at the cinema. What if I'd been with them in the car? What if I could have helped?'

She stood up and stepped in front of him. 'What if you'd been killed too? I hate to say it, Nathan, but the car was crumpled. If you'd been in the back you wouldn't have stood a chance. Charlie would have lost you all.' Her anxious voice quietened. 'I would have lost you all.'

He responded immediately, his bright green eyes locking with hers, the anger dissipating from his voice. This time it was quiet. 'But you lost us all anyway, Rachel. Or we lost you.'

The two of them stood in silence and looked at each other. She could see every weathered line on his face. She understood now. She understood his complete frustration. That was why he'd stayed with Doctors Without Borders. Nathan was all about saving people. He hadn't been able to save the people he'd loved the most—so he tried to make up for it by saving others. And she felt as if she'd compounded it all by walking away when she was ill.

And he was still handsome. He would still turn any woman's head. But he was worn out. He'd reached the end of his emotional tether.

Something curled inside her. What if she hadn't left? What if she'd told him about her renal cancer and stayed with him? How would Nathan have reacted if he hadn't been able to save her either?

She'd spent most of last night tossing and turning, wondering if she'd done the wrong thing. Maybe she should have told Nathan? Maybe she should have stayed to help out with Charlie? It was so easy to have regrets now. She'd lived. She was a cancer survivor and had come out the other side. Because she had the gift of life again, she could easily spend the rest of her time asking *What if?*

But eight years ago she hadn't known that. She hadn't been able to take that chance. Would her treatment in the UK have been as successful as her treatment in Australia? She would never know that.

Even though she'd only been there for a little while, she'd hoped she'd helped Nathan and Charlie deal with their parents' death. Now, she was beginning to realise just how wrong she'd been. None of it was over for Nathan. He'd spent the last eight years consumed by guilt because he hadn't been able to save the people he loved.

He'd spent the last eight years trying to save everyone else.

A horrible feeling crept over her. Just how broken would Nathan have been if he couldn't have saved her either? She shifted uncomfortably and swallowed. She reached for his hand, giving it a little squeeze. She was full of regrets—full of emotion she couldn't even begin to fathom. 'We lost each other,' she said sadly.

Her breath came out in a little shudder. She needed to step away from Nathan again. It didn't matter that he looked muscular and strong. Now, she was realising that, with her strong and smart Nathan, appearances were deceptive.

A wave of fear came over her. In the back of her

mind she'd had the tiniest flicker of hope. Hope that something could rekindle between them. Hope that she could feel a little of the magic she'd felt before with Nathan. It could be so perfect if she could just capture that again.

But her insides were turning over. She felt sick. All of a sudden she could see how damaged and worn down the guy she loved had become. With every tiny line and crease on his face she could see his pain, see how much he'd tried to patch himself back together. And in a way she'd contributed to all this.

Five years. She'd passed the golden five-year point for being cancer-free. But somehow it would always hang over her head. There would always be the possibility, however remote, that it could come back. What if she formed a relationship with Nathan again and had a recurrence?

It had always been in the back of her mind. But she'd tried to be so positive, tried to be so focused on recovery that she hadn't allowed any room in her mind for those kind of thoughts.

But as she stood in front of Nathan now she felt herself unravelling. She wasn't just going to have to walk away from Nathan once; she was going to have to do it twice.

What if, for one minute, he was the person she loved—the way that she had always loved Nathan? The way that he might still love her?

She couldn't do it. She hadn't been able to do it before. And she couldn't do it now.

She couldn't take the tiniest chance that her cancer might return and she could destroy the man she loved.

Before, she hadn't been afraid. She'd been on her own. Any future relationship that might develop would be based on the foundation that she was a cancer survivor.

Now, standing in front of Nathan, she was terrified.

She wanted to love him. She wanted to hold him. She wanted his big strong arms wrapped around her with the feel of his skin next to hers. She wanted to run the palms of her hands over his short hair. She wanted to feel his breath on her neck, the beating of his heart against her own.

But the realisation of how he'd suffered over the last few years was too hard. He'd spent the last five years trying to save the world. It couldn't be done. It could never be done. But it seemed, for Nathan, that was the only thing that healed him. His only redemption.

She reached out and touched his face, letting her fingertips come into contact with his cheek. 'I had no idea,' she whispered. 'I had no idea that's how you felt.' She spoke softly. 'Your parents had a horrible, hideous accident. There was nothing you could have done, Nathan. There was nothing anyone could have done.' Her fingers moved gently down his cheek. 'I'm so sorry I couldn't stay to help you work through this.' Her voice was shaking now. 'But look at the work you've done. Look at the lives you've saved, Nathan.' She gave her head a shake as tears sprang to her eyes. 'It's a horrible thing to say, but if your parents hadn't died—if I hadn't had the cancer diagnosis—things would have been different. We both know that. But who would have saved those lives, Nathan? Who would have made a difference to the kids you've helped through Doctors Without Borders?' As the tears slid down her cheeks she let herself smile. 'Maybe you've saved the next Louis Pasteur or Edward Jenner? Maybe, if you hadn't been there, they wouldn't have been saved?'

She pulled her hand back. It was too tempting. It was too tempting just to step forward and wrap her arms around his neck. To turn her lips towards his.

But she couldn't. She couldn't dare risk that.

He was shaking his head, his green eyes fixed on her. As she breathed he licked his lips and his pupils dilated a little.

She took a tiny step back. 'I have no idea about fate, Nathan. But I have to believe that things happen for a reason. Otherwise, I would be lost in the fact that too many good people are taken much too soon. I have to believe that you went to the places you were supposed to, and saved the people that you should.'

He looked so confused. It was almost as if a little scattering of lights had switched on behind his eyes. He was finally starting to realise how he'd been living. 'But what about you? What about us? What did we do that meant we had to be apart?'

She could almost feel a fist inside her chest grip

her heart and squeeze it tight. 'I don't know,' she whispered. Her feet edged back further.

She could so easily slip. She could so easily tell him how she'd never stopped loving him and wanted to try again. She could so easily tell him that she'd thought about him every day for the last eight years.

But now the cancer seemed like a black cloud above her. If Nathan loved and lost her again, what would that do to him?

It was best to keep things platonic. No matter what her brain and body said about that. She could almost feel the little portcullis slide down in her brain—cutting off her emotions from the rest of her. It took her to a safe place and stopped her from thinking about the things that could break her heart.

She straightened her back and wiped a tear from her cheek.

'What happened when you got to Australia?' he asked. 'What happened with you and Darius?'

Her head dropped. He hadn't put the pieces together yet. He would at some point. But she'd passed the point of keeping secrets from Nathan.

She could trust him. She knew that now beyond a shadow of a doubt. This wasn't about her and Darius. This had never been about her and Darius.

'Ask me how I met him,' she said steadily.

Nathan moved. He set his glass down on the sand and held his hand out towards her. She put her palm in his, letting herself revel in the delicious sensations tingling up towards her shoulder. Her glass was still in her hand as she stepped forward, pressing the whole of her body up against his and wrapping her arm holding the glass around the back of his neck. His hands settled on her hips. The tension in the air between them was palpable.

It was as if they'd waited eight years to have this conversation. It was as if they'd waited eight years to finally be in this place, at this time.

'Rach, how did you meet him?' There was the tiniest tremor in his voice.

The tears flowed. 'I met Darius at the cancer treatment centre,' she whispered.

He froze, his fingers tightening around her waist. For a few seconds their eyes were just locked together in the darkening light. She could see everything on his face. The realisation. The acknowledgement. The recognition.

She could read everything he was thinking— the secrets, the paper-thin medical file.

'Is Darius well? Should he even be here?'

It was the doctor in him. He'd gone from seeing Darius as a rival to seeing him as a patient.

'He had non-Hodgkin's lymphoma. He's relapsed twice over the last few years. As far as I know, he's well right now.'

She could sense him start to relax a little. She licked her lips. 'Darius was never really my boyfriend. We leaned on each other while we were undergoing treatment. I was his sounding board. I knew how to keep a secret. I've never betrayed his trust. That's why he wanted me here. That's the only reason he wanted me here.'

He nodded and reached up, brushing the tears from one cheek, then the other. He didn't ask her any questions. He seemed to instantly respect her explanation.

His anger towards Darius seemed to disappear in the sea winds. It was easy now he knew why she'd been keeping secrets from him. Now, it seemed his only focus was on her.

'Rachel?' he whispered. His fingers ran up her arm to her shoulder and he cradled her cheek in the palm of his hand. 'What next?'

Her blood was warming every part of her skin. This was exactly what she remembered. Exactly what she'd dreamed of. She remembered every part of him. His muscles had changed slightly; they were a bit more defined and a bit more angular. But her body still melded against his the way it always had done. They fitted together. That was how it was with a soulmate. That was the way it was supposed to be.

No one had ever felt as perfect next to her.

She let out a little sob as his hands brushed over her skin. She'd waited for this moment for eight years. She'd spent days and nights dreaming about this.

Dreaming about the moment she would be in Nathan's arms again and she could act on instinct.

He knew now. He knew everything. And although he'd initially been angry, now he had the full picture it seemed he felt exactly the same way she did. They might have been separated by continents, years, accidents and disease but their spark had never died. Their attraction had never died.

His hands were busy, reacquainting themselves with her body. It was like butterflies dancing on her skin. 'This could get wet,' he whispered as her hand slipped and a splash of wine landed on his shoulder. She laughed and stepped back, unwinding her arm and finishing what was left of the wine.

The sea was dark, with a few burnished orange beams from the setting sun scattering across it. This time of night it would be cold. But her skin was so heated she didn't care.

All she felt right now was relief. Relief that she could finally reconnect with the man she'd always wanted.

'Fancy getting completely wet?' she taunted. She set the wine glass down on the sand and held out her hand towards him as his eyes widened.

He didn't hesitate; he put his hand in hers and pulled her towards the water. Nathan wasn't shy.

His T-shirt was pulled over his head in seconds and his shorts dropped on the beach. Rachel didn't need to do that. Her bikini was in place and she left the sheer kaftan covering her hips.

The water chilled her thighs as they strode out into the dark sea. Once they'd reached waist height Nathan turned around and grabbed her. She didn't wait for a second. Talking wasn't what she wanted to do right now.

The chilled water hadn't stilled the thudding of her heartbeat. As Nathan's hands pulled her closer the buoyancy of the water let her wrap her legs around his waist.

His lips came into contact with hers. It was what she'd been waiting for. Since they'd kissed yesterday. Since she'd walked away eight years ago.

And the promise of his lips hadn't changed. He didn't just kiss her. He devoured her. It was everything she remembered. It was everything that had haunted her dreams for the last eight years.

Nathan's lips had been made for hers. And she remembered exactly why they'd been so good together. Her hands curled around his head, brushing his buzz cut, feeling the bristles under her palm. His hands ran through her hair; one hand anchored her head in place whilst his lips worked his way around her neck and shoulders and his other hand was held against her bottom.

The waves continued to buffet them, pulling them one way, then the other. Every current pulled them even closer together, his hard muscles against her softer curves.

Now his hands moved lower, swiftly grabbing the bottom of her kaftan and pulling it over her head. It disappeared into the waves.

His hands were back on her bare skin, cradling her and pulling her tighter towards him. The chilled water did nothing to hide his response to her.

She leaned back a little and ran her palms up the planes of his chest. His years in Doctors Without Borders had left him leaner, more muscular. It was understandable. The places where he'd served would have required long hours and hard labour. Nathan wouldn't have shirked any of that.

Something pinged. The snap on her bikini top

sprang apart and the cold water rushed underneath the pink Lycra. It billowed between them and was swallowed by the sea as his fingers brushed against her nipple.

Even in the dark she could see his green eyes on hers. Her teeth grazed the nape of his neck as she kissed even harder. He started walking, striding back towards the beach with her legs still wound around his waist. 'Let's take this back to land,' he said.

This time his hands fitted firmly around her waist, anchoring her in place. This time the pads of his fingers came in contract with the curved scar on her back. This time she had no cover. The bikini top and kaftan were lost amongst the waves. He inhaled sharply.

It was a jarring reminder of the gulf between them.

He fixed her with a stare she hadn't seen before—one of wariness—as he set her down. Then he didn't speak. He just moved her gently to one side, pushing her onto one hip.

She was holding her breath as he gently traced his finger down the curve of her scar. Her chest was hurting, struggling under the strain of little oxygen. Her stomach churned. She had no idea what he would do, what he would say.

But, as she let the breath whoosh out from her chest, he took it away all over again. He bent and gently brushed his lips against her scar.

His voice was husky. 'You should have told me, Rach. You should always have told me.'

His voice was cracking. She could see his emotions written on his face. It was breaking her heart all over again.

She hadn't stayed around the last time to witness this. Last time around she'd witnessed his shock, disbelief and then a little bit of anger. She knew exactly what she'd done to him. She just hadn't waited around for the fallout.

This time it was right in front of her. The hurt, the confusion, the sadness. This was why she hadn't stayed. She couldn't have stood this. She just wasn't strong enough for this.

Her voice was cracking. 'I always think I messed up. But I did the best thing in the circumstances. Even though I regret it every single day.'

Suddenly she felt swamped. Swamped by what

had just happened between them, and confused by it even more.

She'd been so caught up in the fantasy of this. For a few moments, the beautiful setting and the man in front of her had just swept her away. But his lips connecting with her scar brought her back to the harsh reality of life and the decisions that she'd made.

She'd wished for this for the last eight years. But now it was right in front of her she couldn't let herself go. She couldn't lose herself in the moment with Nathan because of the multitude of fears she still had. The rational parts of her brain were telling her to move on. She was past the five-year cancer-free mark.

Now was the time to think about a new relationship and maybe even see if she could revive her dream of having a family.

But some part of her heart just couldn't let her take that final step.

The hurt on his face had been a painful reminder of what she'd already put him through. She didn't want to take the chance of hurting Nathan more than she already had.

Everything had happened too soon for her. Her brain really hadn't had time to process how she felt about all this. She needed some time. She needed some space.

Above all, right now, she felt as if she needed to get away. Needed to get away from the man she still loved with her whole heart.

She jumped up and made a grab for his T-shirt that was lying on the sand. 'I'm sorry, Nathan. I can't. I just can't.'

Confusion racked his face. 'What? What are you talking about?'

She waved her hand. 'This. It's all just too much, too soon. I need some time to think about things.' Her feet were already moving across the sand. Back towards the cabin. Back towards safety.

'Rachel, wait!' He jumped to his feet as if to come after her but she put up her hand.

'No, Nathan. If you care about me at all, you'll give me some space. We haven't seen each other in eight years. *Eight years, Nathan.* There's so much unfinished business between us. I can't straighten out how I feel about everything.'

She was still walking.

'Do you love me, Rachel?'

His voice cut through the sea wind and stopped her cold.

She turned again, but the words were stuck in her throat. Of course she loved him—she'd never stopped. She just wasn't ready to say that yet. She could never guarantee that she'd be healthy. She could never guarantee her cancer wouldn't come back. Was she brave enough to expose him to that? Was she brave enough to expose *them* to that? It was all about trust again. Could she trust their potential relationship to see them through anything? She just wasn't sure.

'Because I love you, Rachel. I'll always love you. I've spent so much time being bitter. I've spent so much time being angry about my parents dying. I've never stepped back to see how much it impacted on my life—on Charlie's life.' He gave a little laugh. 'It turns out my little brother is more of a man than I ever thought. He's got past it—he's moved on. He's found love. He's got a family. And I envy him every single day.' He emphasised those words as he stepped towards her.

But he didn't reach out and touch her. He kept his hands by his sides. 'You've had cancer, Rachel. It's time for you to move on too. It's time for both of us to move on.' He took a deep breath. 'But I'll give you time. I'll give you space. You need to get to the same place as me. The one where you can say that you're ready to love me again.'

He let the words hang in the air between them.

The sky was dark. She was too far away to see the expression on his face. All she could feel was an invisible weight pressing down on her chest.

Her head was so jammed full of thoughts that she just needed to get away. So, before he could say anything else, she turned on her heel and ran.

Ran as fast as she could along the beach and back to the cabin, slamming the door behind her and heading straight to her bed.

She had to make a decision. She had to try and find a way to think straight.

Because right now she just couldn't.

CHAPTER TEN

'HOW MANY TIMES has he refilled that water bottle?'

Nathan was watching the monitor that was fixed on the camp. Camp life was boring. There was no getting away from it. The director had spent most of the day trying to stage a fight between two of the celebrities.

And Nathan had spent the last two days trying to avoid Rachel.

Part of him thought that giving into the undeniable chemistry between them might have diminished the tension between them. He couldn't have been more wrong.

There was nothing like being stranded on an island with your ex for increasing tension to epic proportions—particularly after what had just happened between them.

Part of him felt sick. Rachel—*his Rachel*—had suffered from renal cancer.

His brain couldn't get past the part that she hadn't told him.

But now… *Now* he had a reason why she'd left. And the lack of trust was hard to stomach. But with a bit more thinking time and a bit more reason he could almost understand why she'd thought she was doing the right thing.

He still believed she had been wrong. The thought of Rachel having cancer might burn a hole inside him, but now the fact that she *hadn't* walked away because she didn't love him—as crazy as it sounded—that part was almost a relief.

That part had preyed on his mind constantly. He'd always wondered why she'd done it. Now there was a reason. She said she'd loved him too much. She said she'd walked away *because* she loved him. He still couldn't quite get his head around that.

The other night had been an epiphany for him. He'd stood on the beach and known that, no matter how he felt or how angry he'd been, he would always love her. Always. He'd always want her in his life.

The feelings were so overwhelming that he'd understood when she'd said she needed time. Now he'd found Rachel again, he didn't want her to slip through his fingers. Not again.

Parts of his heart still squirmed, his self-defence mechanism wanting to kick into place and stop him from being vulnerable. How on earth would he feel if Rachel walked away from him again? It was almost unthinkable.

But it could happen. And if he considered it too much he would simply turn and walk away himself. Eight years was a long time. They'd both changed so much. Niggling doubts were creeping in because Rachel hadn't been able to look him in the eye and say for sure what she wanted. He was taking a huge risk.

He'd survived her walking away once—but what about twice?

He took a deep breath and focused on the screen in front of him. He was here to do a job. Other parts of his life would have to wait. He asked the question again. 'How many times has he refilled that water bottle?'

The technician looked up from the monitor and frowned, breaking him from his thoughts. 'Three—maybe four times? He spends most of his day in the dunny too.' He paused. 'Or sleeping.'

Nathan ran his fingers over his buzz cut. The dunny—the Australian equivalent of a toilet. He'd even used the word himself the other day. Darius was drinking too much and peeing frequently. Something was wrong. He was in doctor mode now. He had to stop focusing on Rachel. His gut instinct told him that something wasn't right here. It didn't help that now he knew Darius's medical history he was even more worried. There was no getting away from the fact the guy just didn't *look* well.

He hated to admit it, but Darius was generally a good-looking guy—well-built, with dark hair, tanned skin and a movie star smile. He was kind of surprised the guy had stayed in a soap opera in Australia and not tried to hit Hollywood.

He watched as Darius tugged at his shorts,

pulling them up. His weight loss had been evident the first time Nathan had seen him. Now, it was even more marked. And if the clothes he'd brought with him were falling off—it was time to act.

Nathan walked over to the director's chair. 'Darius Cornell. Get him out of there. I want to check him over.'

The director looked up. 'What are you talking about? Darius is fine. He hasn't complained about anything.' He looked at the rest of the people in the cabin. 'Has he?'

The ones that were listening shook their heads. The director held up his hands. 'See?'

Nathan leaned on the desk and pointed at the screen. 'Does that guy look well to you?'

The director glanced back at the screen and hesitated. 'He has been going to the dunny a lot. Maybe he has one of those parasitic bugs? Maybe he's picked up something in the jungle?' Unconsciously, the director started to scratch his skin.

Nathan put his hand on the man's shoulder. 'Leave the diagnosing to me. Can you send someone to get him out of there for a quick check over?' He looked around. There was no getting away from it—he couldn't avoid her for ever. 'And could someone find Dr Johnson and ask her to report to the medical cabin?'

He didn't wait for an answer, just walked back to the medical centre and tried to keep everything in his head in check.

Rachel and Darius in a room together. For the first time since he'd got here he couldn't care less. Now he knew Darius's history, he was worried about him—really worried. If the guy was having a third recurrence of his non-Hodgkin's it couldn't possibly be good.

It only took a few minutes for Darius to arrive and he was less than happy to see Nathan. 'What are you doing here? I thought I made it clear I'd only deal with Rachel.'

Nathan held up Darius's empty medical file. 'Rachel will be along soon. I'm worried about you, Darius. You don't look well. You can't possibly feel well. How much weight do you think you've lost?'

Darius scowled at him as he sat down in a chair and started scratching at his skin.

But Nathan wasn't going to let this go. He wasn't about to betray what Rachel had revealed to him but he had to get to the bottom of what was wrong. 'Darius, let's not play games. What I need to know right now is what your symptoms are. I'm worried about you.'

Darius blinked—as if a whole host of thoughts had just flooded his brain—and Nathan heard a sharp intake of breath behind him. Rachel.

'What's going on?' She walked straight in. 'Darius? Is something wrong?'

Darius, who normally spent his time trying to charm everyone around him, was unusually bad-tempered. 'Don't ask me—ask him. It was him that pulled me out of the jungle.'

'With good reason,' cut in Nathan.

'What have you told him, Rach?' Darius looked mad.

Nathan's eyes fell on the water canister that Darius still held in his hands. He hadn't even put it down when he'd been called to the medical cabin. He obviously had a raging thirst. The question was—why?

Nathan took a deep breath and leaned against

the desk. He tried not to fixate on Rachel in her unusual get-up of pink sundress, thick socks and hiking boots. He'd no idea where she'd been. But he could almost feel her brown eyes burrowing into the side of his head.

She paused at the doorway, taking in the situation in front of her. In the unflinching bright lights of the medical centre it was obvious that Darius was unwell. She walked towards him. 'I haven't told Nathan anything—but I'm just about to.' Her eyes met Nathan's, a silent thank you for not exposing what she'd already revealed. 'He's the doctor on duty and he needs the full facts. Darius and I met when we both had cancer treatment. I had renal cancer and Darius had non-Hodgkin's lymphoma. He's relapsed twice since.'

Darius glared at Rachel and gritted his teeth. But he didn't speak.

Nathan tried again. 'Darius, tell me honestly—how are you feeling? Because, to be frank—you look like crap.'

Rachel's eyebrows shot upwards and Darius almost growled at him. He stood back up and pushed himself into Nathan's face. 'Who do you think you're talking to?'

And with that simple act Nathan's suspicions were confirmed. Darius's breath smelled of pear drops—something Nathan hadn't tasted since he was a child. It was a classic sign of diabetes and that, combined with all the other signs, probably meant that he was in ketoacidosis. Onset could be really rapid. He put his hand gently on Darius's arm and steered him back towards the chair, walking over to the cupboard and pulling out a glucometer. Rachel's eyes widened for a second and he could almost see the jigsaw pieces falling into place for her.

'Darius, I need to do a little test on you. It's just a finger prick; I'll squeeze out a little blood and we'll know what we need to know in ten seconds.'

'No.' Darius's aggression wasn't lessening but it wasn't him; it was his condition.

Nathan sat down opposite while Rachel moved over and kneeled in front of Darius. She put her hand on Darius's water canister. 'How much have you been drinking?'

He automatically took a swig from the bottle. 'I'm just thirsty.'

She nodded. 'And have you been going to the toilet a lot?'

'Well, I would. I'm drinking a lot.' He was snappy.

She reached over and took the glucometer from Nathan's hands. 'You've lost weight, Darius. More than we would have expected in the jungle. I think you might be suffering from diabetes. Let me do this little test.'

She was quick. He barely had a chance to reply before she'd done the little finger prick. The machine counted down rapidly and she grimaced and turned it to face Nathan.

She put her arm behind Darius and stood him up, leading him over to the examination trolley. 'We're going to set up a drip. Your body is dehydrated. Do you know what diabetes is?'

He scowled. 'Of course I do. My mum had it, remember?'

Nathan could see the flicker across Rachel's face. She remembered now. And diabetes could be hereditary. He should be feeling a little more relaxed. They had a diagnosis for Darius. Nathan looked through the drawers and pulled out a cannula and an IV giving set. It only took a few seconds to find a drip stand and a bag of saline. Rachel was an experienced medical physician. She must have looked after plenty of newly diagnosed diabetics. The condition was becoming more prevalent across the world. He'd certainly diagnosed it often in his time with Doctors Without Borders.

He walked around the other side of Darius and quickly inserted the cannula while Rachel was still talking.

'This is serious, Darius. We don't have a lot of facilities here. I'd like to transfer you to a hospital. That's the best place for you to be right now. We need to get some insulin into you and stabilise your condition. Once you're stabilised you'll feel a lot better. It only takes a couple of days.'

'I'm not going to hospital.' The words were sharp.

He saw her take a deep breath. Being unreasonable was right in there with the rest of the symptoms for diabetes, along with weight loss, drinking too much, peeing frequently and the acidotic breath.

He pulled out his stethoscope and tried to place it on Darius's chest but he batted his hand away. Nathan didn't even blink. He just calmly put his fingers on Darius's wrist, checking his pulse rate.

Rachel fixed her eyes on his. He spoke clearly. 'Only slightly tachycardic. Let's check his blood pressure.' He was trying to determine just how near to crisis Darius was.

'Do we have any insulin?'

Nathan nodded. 'There are a few varieties in the drug fridge. But we don't have an insulin pump.'

She gave a little nod and walked quickly to the fridge, unlocking the door and examining the contents. She looked over at Darius. 'You should be in hospital. You need your bloods taken and a few other assessments. You should be on a continuous pump and your blood sugar constantly monitored until we get you stabilised.'

She was saying everything she was supposed to be saying. But Nathan had the strangest feeling this wasn't going to go the way it should. Darius seemed strangely determined.

Darius was looking at her. 'If I go to a regular hospital they'll want to know my medical history. Can't you just give me insulin here and look after me? You do this stuff all the time.'

She shook her head. 'I do this stuff all the time in a general hospital with staff to assist me. I don't have the equipment I need. I can't even do a blood panel on you right now. I would class this as a medical emergency. I think we should call the medevac again.'

Nathan could see the mild panic in her eyes. Part of him understood and part of him didn't. Yes, this was a diabetic crisis. But, as an experienced physician, Rachel could administer the approximate dose of insulin and monitor Darius herself. With the IV in situ to correct his dehydration, it wasn't an ideal situation but it could be managed. There was no question Darius would have to be referred to a diabetic specialist but, in the immediate future, this could be controlled. He'd stabilised lots of newly diagnosed diabetics with far less equipment than they had here.

Nowadays, for most patients, they tried to avoid admission to hospital unless they were at crisis point and instead had them attend a day care centre.

Nathan took a deep breath. Things were still raw between them both. And padding round about Rachel's ex wouldn't help. But he was rational enough to know that Darius was a patient. He had a right to make requests about his treatment.

It was time to get down to basics. He turned to face Darius. 'Why is it you don't want to go to a hospital? Is it because of your medical history—or because of the show?'

'The show,' Darius said without hesitation. 'It's in the contract that if I leave early—medical condition or not—I won't get my full salary. I promised Lynn she'd get her dream wedding. If I don't stay, I won't be able to do that.' He still sounded angry. He was still agitated. The condition was impacting every part of his body.

Nathan glanced at Rachel. She'd told him Darius was engaged to someone else but this was the first time he'd heard Darius mention his fiancée.

Rachel was still frowning. 'We need a set of scales.' She was moving out of panic mode and into doctor mode.

Nathan found the scales and brought them around to the side of the trolley where the drip was. He helped Darius stand up for a few seconds and took a note. He gestured towards the medical file. 'Do we have his weight when he first arrived?'

She flicked through a few pages. 'We have one—from the insurance medical.' She looked at the records. 'It was done just over a month ago. According to the scales now he's lost ten pounds.'

Nathan nodded and touched Darius's arm. 'Do you know what kind of diabetes your mother had?'

'She had it from childhood and was always on insulin. That's Type One, isn't it?'

He nodded. 'From your symptoms, it's likely that's what you have too.' He glanced at Rachel. 'Agree?'

She nodded as she dialled up the dosage on an insulin pen. 'We'll need a GAD test for confirmation but that's the way we'll treat it right now. We need to get your blood glucose levels down.'

Darius leaned back against the pillow on the trolley. 'I want to speak to the director. I want to go back into camp. But—' he closed his eyes for a second '—can I sleep for a bit first?'

Rachel gave a little tap at his abdomen. 'Pull up your shirt. I'm going to give you the first shot of insulin. Then I'm going to take some bloods and see if we can find a way to get them onshore. We need to keep doing the finger prick tests. Feel free to try and sleep through them.'

She gave him the insulin, then spent two minutes taking blood from inside his elbow. Nathan picked up the phone and spoke for a few minutes to one of the crew. He gave her a nod. 'The supply boat is due in an hour. They'll make special arrangements for the bloods.' He took the vials and stuck them in a transport container.

He hesitated and looked over as she scribbled some notes. Darius already looked as if he was sleeping. 'I'll grab us some coffee and we can have a chat about how best to handle this outside.'

* * *

Rachel's stomach was in knots. Everything that could go wrong had gone wrong. She couldn't believe it when she'd got the call about Darius and now she was kicking herself that she hadn't investigated sooner.

When she'd walked in, she'd thought he'd had a relapse. Seeing him in the bright lights of the medical cabin rather than the shaded canopy of the jungle had been a shock to the system. His skin pallor was terrible, the dehydration obvious and the weight loss evident on his face.

But knowing that it was diabetes and not a recurrence of his non-Hodgkin's lymphoma was a relief.

Diabetes she could manage. Nathan was right. She was an experienced physician—as was he. As long as she had insulin and glucose monitoring equipment they could stabilise him in a few days. His long-term care would have to be monitored by a diabetes specialist but there was no reason she couldn't manage his immediate care.

She'd just gone into shock when she'd first realised something was wrong. It had taken her a few minutes to calm down and be rational. She gave a little smile. Darius did have his good points. It was sweet that he wanted to see out his contract in order to give Lynn her dream wedding. He wasn't as self-obsessed as some might think. And the nice part was that she knew if Lynn heard that he'd done this she'd be furious in case he'd put himself at risk. They really were a devoted couple.

Nathan walked up and handed her a mug. The coffee aroma swept around her, along with something else. Hazelnut. Somewhere on this island Nathan had found her favourite drink—a hazelnut latte. He didn't even wait for her to speak. 'We have a patient to look after.'

She was surprised—surprised that he hadn't even mentioned what had happened a few nights ago. He'd said he'd give her space, and he had. She just wasn't sure that she'd entirely believed him that night. But Nathan had been true to his word. She'd never seen him alone since.

And now it felt as if he'd been avoiding her. Her stomach curled. She was sure he must regret saying those words to her. Telling her that he still loved her—that he'd always loved her. She hadn't reciprocated, even though she'd wanted to. It must have felt like a slap to the face. What would happen when he found out what her plans were? She didn't even want to go there.

She lifted her head. 'Yes. Darius…'

His shoulders set and there was a flicker along his jawline. 'How do you want to handle this?'

Work. She could talk about work. She could talk about a diabetes plan for Darius. 'I'll stay with him for the next few hours, monitoring his blood sugar. If he needs more insulin I'll talk him through doing an injection. I've no idea what his consultant's plan will be for him, but he's got to start somewhere. Might as well be here.'

Nathan nodded and placed his hands on his hips. At least he was being professional—at least he was being courteous. Then his green eyes looked right at her and she felt a jolt right through her system. 'What do you want me to do?'

What do you want me to do? She could answer that question and give him a dozen different variables that were nothing to do with diabetes.

But she was trying not to think about Nathan

Banks, the man. She was trying only to think of Nathan Banks, the fellow health professional.

She tried to clear her head and be rational. 'I'd appreciate it if you could speak to the director and work out a plan so Darius can go back into camp for a few hours every day. Just for the camera. The director will need to tell the other campmates what's happened. And he'll need to agree to one of us being there.'

Nathan gave a sharp nod. 'I can do that. What about you? Do you want me to take over at some point? We'll still need to supervise the other challenges.'

She hesitated. She already knew that Darius wouldn't like it. But she had to be realistic. She could probably wake every few hours and monitor Darius's blood sugar, but she couldn't keep doing that for ever. It made more sense to spread the load.

'I want to try and get him back to normal as much as we can. How about we assess him later and, if he's up to it, he could walk to the canteen with you for dinner?'

He tried his best to hide the tiny grimace that

she could see flicker across his face. 'Fine. I'll speak to the director and be back around six.'

He turned on his heel and walked away as she leaned against the doorjamb. She still had the coffee cup clenched in one hand and it crumpled beneath her fingers, sending the remainder of the coffee spilling down her pink dress.

She wanted to cry again. She wanted to go into her room, get into her bed, curl up in a ball and just cry.

Everything just felt like too much. Just being on this island felt like too much. The fact that Darius was sick. The fact that, after all these years, she could see the damage that had been done to Nathan—the man she still loved.

That tore at her heart most of all. Her barriers were breaking, her walls were crumbling. At work, if things got tough, you could always retreat to the sanctity of your own home. But there was nowhere to retreat to on this island.

There would always be someone there—a crew member or a camera to make you realise how little space there was. And now, with all the emotions—and the secrets she was trying to keep—there wasn't even room for her own thoughts.

All of a sudden she couldn't wait to get away from this place. It might be an island paradise for some, but for her it had turned into something entirely different.

How many more days could she try to avoid the man she had to work with? How many more days would she have to push aside everything she felt for him? This place was rapidly becoming unbearable.

For a tiny second she even considered phoning Lewis and telling him he had to get his butt out here so she could leave.

But she couldn't do that. His wife would be anxious enough waiting for her baby without her husband disappearing at short notice.

There was a cough behind her and she spun around. Darius was rubbing his eyes and sitting up a little.

'How are you feeling?' She dumped the crumpled cup in the bin and walked over to him.

His brow creased and he pointed at her stained

dress. 'How long have I been asleep and what have you been doing?'

She shook her head. 'Nothing. Nothing at all. Now, let's get your blood sugar tested again and see if we can start to make you feel better.' She adjusted the flow rate on the drip and reached for the glucometer.

Doctor business. She could do this. She'd always been good at her job and at least if she was thinking about Darius she wasn't thinking about anyone else.

She quickly pricked his finger and waited ten seconds to see the result. She pasted a smile on her face. 'It's coming down slowly. What say I get some insulin and teach you how to do the next injection?'

She straightened her back. She had to start thinking about herself. 'Then we need to have a chat. I've made a decision I need to tell you about.'

CHAPTER ELEVEN

IT WAS MORE than a little awkward. Nathan didn't want to be there any more than Darius wanted him to be.

But they'd walked slowly down to the canteen together and were now sitting across from each other while Darius stirred his soup round and round.

There was no getting away from the fact the guy looked bad. His face was gaunt and there were big dark circles under his eyes. If he had any idea how he looked he'd probably be shouting for a mirror and make-up.

But Nathan could tell that Darius was just too tired. It was all part and parcel of the diagnosis of diabetes. The extreme fatigue would lift in a few days and his muscles would start to rebuild. Within a month he should look normal again. He still had an excessive thirst—he'd drunk three glasses of water since they'd sat down—but his appetite had obviously left him.

Nathan took a deep breath and let his professional head stay in place. 'You going to eat that? You've just taken another shot. You don't want to end up the other way and let your blood sugar go too low.'

Darius let out something equivalent to a growl and finally lifted the spoon to his lips. His eyes were fixed firmly on Nathan. There was clearly a mixture of resentment and curiosity in them. It seemed these feelings worked both ways.

'So, you're the famous Nathan Banks,' he finally said.

Nathan felt an uncomfortable prickle down his spine. He tried his best to be calm. 'I don't know what you mean.'

Darius lifted his eyelids just a touch. 'It took me a while to realise exactly who you were. You were her favourite topic of conversation.'

He was? The thought of Rachel and her then new boyfriend discussing him didn't sit well.

'I would have thought I was the last thing you'd want to talk about.'

Darius sat back and folded his arms across his chest. It was apparent he wanted to direct this conversation. 'You're not as good-looking as I thought you'd be.'

Nathan didn't know whether to laugh or punch him. This clearly wasn't a doctor-patient conversation any more.

He set his fork down. It was clear they wouldn't be eating any time soon. 'Really.' It wasn't a question; it was a statement of fact.

Darius shook his head. 'No. I saw a picture of you once. Rachel kept it in her bag.' He gave a little half-smile. 'Time obviously hasn't been kind to you.'

Nathan shook his head. On any other day of the week, in any other set of circumstances he'd probably knock Darius out cold. But this guy was clearly trying to play him. And he had no idea why. The thought that Rachel had kept a picture of him in her bag was sending strange pulses through his body. But this wasn't the time to get all nostalgic.

He countered. 'Botox has clearly been kind to you.'

He couldn't help it. Even though he hated to admit it, Darius was normally a good-looking guy, with tanned skin and perfectly straight white teeth. Nathan was quite sure that with his weather-beaten skin and lines around his eyes he'd come up short in comparison.

He just couldn't help the fact that everything about this guy annoyed him. His hair, his skin, his teeth—even the way he ate. If Darius Cornell had been your average soap star Nathan wouldn't have cared less. But Darius Cornell was the soap star who had dated Rachel and that made his insides feel as if they were curling up and dying inside and gave him a completely irrational hatred of the guy.

He was trying so hard to put Darius in the 'patient' box in his head. That would help him try to keep everything professional. But then he'd go and say something about Rachel and all rational thoughts went out of the window.

He knew. He knew why they'd been friends. He just hadn't managed to push all the ideas that had fixated in his head over the years out of the way yet.

Because in his mind Rachel Johnson was still his.

In his mind, Rachel would always be his.

The other night he'd acted on instinct; he'd put his heart before his head and just told her that he still loved her. So many things she'd said had set off little pulses of recognition in his brain.

He *had* spent the last five years trying to save the world. Even if he hadn't realised it at the time. No one could do that. No one. All his pent-up frustration about his mum and dad had been channelled into his job. In that respect, it was time for change. It was time to re-evaluate and decide where he wanted to be. There was a tiny idea flickering in the back of his mind.

But, in other respects, things were exactly the same. Eight years on, nothing had changed.

Eight years on, he still loved Rachel Johnson.

Darius was still studying him as the feeling started to fully form in his brain.

'I always wondered what you were like,' Darius said. His tone was verging on disparaging.

'Why should you care what I was like? I was

in England. You were the one in Australia—with her.'

For a few seconds Darius's gaze was still locked on his. It must be the actor in him. The overwhelming confidence. But Nathan wouldn't break the stare. It was almost like marking his line in the sand.

He didn't want anyone else to have any claim on Rachel.

Darius sucked in a deep breath. 'But Rachel was never really with me,' he muttered quietly. 'You were the one she was always thinking of.' His shoulders sagged as if all the wind had gone out of his sails. Maybe he was tired? Maybe he needed to find him something else to eat?

Darius looked up from under his heavy lids, his expression a little glazed. 'Rachel... She was never mine. You were always the person in her head.' He gave a little laugh. 'It does wonders for the confidence. And you're about to lose her all over again.'

The words made his head shoot up and focus. 'What did you say?'

What on earth did Darius mean? He wanted to

give the guy a shake, but as he looked at Darius he realised that right now there was only room for doctor mode. His eyes were glassy. He reached into his back pocket and pulled out the glucometer, not even waiting for Darius's permission. 'You haven't eaten enough. What do you want?'

'Toast.' A one-word answer from someone who obviously wasn't feeling great. Nathan strode across the canteen and walked straight into the kitchen, bypassing the baffled chef. He grabbed a few slices of bread, putting them in the toaster and opening the fridge for some butter and jam.

The chef lifted his eyebrows. 'Help yourself.'

Nathan patted him on the shoulder. 'Sorry, Stan. Darius isn't feeling too well. Just want to get some food into him.'

Stan nodded. 'No worries.' He carried on with his dinner preparations.

After a minute the toast popped and Nathan spread the butter and jam, pouring a glass of milk too. He walked back across the canteen, ignoring the curious stares around him, putting the plate and glass in front of Darius.

He needed this guy to feel well again—he needed to ask him what he'd meant about Rachel.

Darius didn't even look up—he just automatically started eating. After five minutes the glazed expression left him and he sat back in the chair, looking at the empty plate in front of him. His gaze narrowed and he folded his arms across his chest and glanced over his shoulder to check if anyone else was listening. When he was satisfied that the rest of the crew were more interested in their food than listening to anyone else's conversation, he turned back around.

'Do you feel better?'

Darius gave a brief nod. His look was still a little belligerent. But Nathan wasn't prepared to wait a second longer.

He leaned across the table. 'What did you mean about Rachel?'

Darius scowled. 'I was a bit foggy there. I might have said something I didn't mean to.'

'Lots of diabetics say odd things when their blood sugar goes a bit low. But you said something about Rachel. You said I was about to lose her all over again. What did you mean?'

Darius shook his head. 'It's private. Anyway, we should only be discussing doctor stuff.'

Nathan fixed his gaze on Darius and sucked in a deep breath, trying to keep professional. 'We should really discuss how you felt when your blood sugar went down. You need to be able to recognise the signs.' He turned the glucometer around. 'Normal blood sugar is between four and seven. But you've been running much higher in the last few weeks. Your blood sugar was ten. That's obviously the point you start to feel unwell. All that will change, but we need to keep notes.'

There was complete silence for a few seconds.

After a minute Darius stood up and picked up the glucometer. 'I'm feeling a bit better now. I think I'd prefer to discuss the diabetes stuff with Rachel.' He glared at Nathan. 'While I've still got the chance, that is.'

Nathan stood up too. 'You're not going anywhere until you tell me what you mean.'

Darius snapped at him, 'It's all your fault. She's supposed to stay on the island the whole time I'm here. But she's not. She's leaving. She's getting on the next supply boat that arrives the day after tomorrow. And she's doing that to get away from you!'

He turned on his heel and stalked out of the canteen as the bottom fell out of Nathan's world.

No. She couldn't. She couldn't leave him again.

Not Rachel. Not when he finally felt as if there was a real chance of a future together.

He just couldn't let it happen.

CHAPTER TWELVE

THE TV PRODUCER and director had finally listened to reason. Nathan had been surprisingly persuasive. If she hadn't known better, she might have thought that he and Darius were friends.

They'd reached a compromise. Darius was hydrated enough to be off his IV fluids. They'd had his blood results sent back and spoken to a diabetic specialist about a treatment regime. Rachel would start his treatment, then, as soon as filming was finished, Darius would fly back to the mainland for a proper consultation.

He'd been quietly amenable. The background information he already knew about diabetes had been helpful. But treatments and plans had changed a lot since his mother had been diagnosed and Rachel was keen to make sure he got the best information.

The trickiest part had been the other celebrities.

The phrase 'special treatment' had been readily bandied about. Nathan had ended up in the middle of the camp telling them straight how crucial it was for Darius to be monitored during these first few days. He would only be back in camp for a few hours each day for filming. The rest of the time he'd be monitored and recuperating in the crew area. Tallie Turner, the actress, had been the most disgruntled. The thought of someone else sleeping on anything other than a lumpy camp bed, away from the spiders and bugs, was obviously too much for her.

The rest of the celebrities had spent most of the day talking about it. Frank Cairns, the sportsman, was proving the public's obvious favourite. He didn't get involved in griping, rarely tolerated tantrums and had a real, self-deprecating sense of humour. Most of the votes in the last few days had been for him. Billy X, the rapper, was the second most popular. He'd done well in the challenges and had started a heavy flirtation with Rainbow Blossom, the reality TV star. Rachel was quite sure it was a calculated move for popularity but she wouldn't dream of saying so.

There was only one more day to go. Tomorrow she would be on the supply boat and away from Nathan completely. She still couldn't figure out if that was what she really wanted.

She'd stayed at the medical centre last night with Darius but they'd both agreed that Darius should be allowed to bunk in with some of the crew tonight. One of them would go and wake him to check his blood sugar a few times in the middle of the night, but getting him back to normal as soon as possible was important. If he'd been diagnosed in the city he would maybe have had a one or two nights' stay in hospital if he was close to crisis to stabilise him, then he'd spend the next couple of days with a few hours at day care. All his other follow-ups would be done as an outpatient.

It was time to get things back to normal.

Normal? What was that? Because she didn't know.

Was it normal to wake up every morning and feel sick? Was it normal not to be able to sleep at night because of all the thoughts tumbling around in your brain? Was it normal not to be able to think straight and have a conversation with your colleague?

Normal didn't seem to exist for Rachel Johnson any more. Not since Nathan Banks had reappeared in her life.

Footsteps sounded on the path outside the cabin and her body tensed. She could even recognise his steps now. It was going from bad to worse. Her bed was currently covered with the contents of her wardrobe as she tried to cram them back into her rucksack. What would he say when he noticed? She still hadn't told him she planned to leave.

As she lifted up yet another carefully folded T-shirt she stopped to take a breath. Why had it taken her so long to pack? If she was really desperate to leave the island she should have just shoved everything into her rucksack. Instead, she'd been carefully folding everything, rolling up dresses and skirts. It was almost as if her head had made one decision and her heart another.

Was running away really the answer?

As the footsteps grew closer she squeezed her eyes closed for a second. *This* was what she needed to do. *This* was the conversation she needed to have—no matter how hard. She couldn't walk away from him again without talking to him first.

It wasn't fair to her. It wasn't fair to him.

Eight years ago she'd run away.

Eight years later, it was time to face things head-on.

'Hey, Rach?'

His happy tone took her by surprise. They'd spent the last day tiptoeing around each other and barely making eye contact.

She turned around. He had a bottle in his hand and two champagne glasses. She stood up, forgetting that she was only wearing her short pink satin nightdress. Nathan strode across the cabin and put the bottle on the table. He didn't mention the clothes spread everywhere. 'Look what Lewis sent us. It just arrived on the supply boat.'

Her eyes widened as she spun the bottle around. Pink champagne from the man she planned to kill. It was kind of ironic. Then her brain clicked into gear.

'They've had the baby?'

Nathan was beaming. 'They've had the baby— a happy, healthy eight-pound girl.' He reached over and gave her a spontaneous hug. 'You know he'd been really worried, don't you? Every other female in his wife's family had developed pre-eclampsia while they were pregnant. I think Lewis spent the whole pregnancy holding his breath.'

He was still holding her and she was trying to pretend her body wasn't responding to his touch as his male pheromones flooded around her. The stubble on his chin grazed her shoulder and every tiny hair on her body stood on end. She'd always loved Nathan with stubble.

'No,' she whispered. 'I didn't know that.'

He was holding her gaze, his good mood still evident. This was the Nathan she remembered. This was the Nathan who'd kept her buoyed and supported through six years of hard study and work. This was the guy who made her laugh. This was the guy who she had always trusted, the person she trusted with her heart. Why couldn't she have him back? It was almost as if the little shadows behind his eyes had fallen away. He seemed more relaxed. He seemed at ease with the world around him. And whilst the tension emanating from him had diminished, the pheromones were sparking like fireworks.

He hadn't let her go. And she didn't really want him to.

Maybe for five minutes she could pretend that she'd never had cancer? She could pretend that she'd never left and he'd spent the last five years trying to save the world. Maybe for the next five minutes they could try being happy with each other. She wanted that so badly.

'What's the baby's name?' she asked.

His nose wrinkled. 'Gilberta.'

She pulled back a little. 'What?'

He shrugged. 'Apparently it's a family name.' He glanced over at the champagne on the table. 'What do you say, Rach? Wanna drink some champagne with me?'

His arms released her as he reached over to grab the bottle and she felt the air go out of her with a little whoosh. Nathan didn't notice. He was too busy popping the cork and pouring the bubbling liquid into glasses.

No. She couldn't do this. She couldn't keep living this life. If you'd asked her a few weeks ago about Nathan Banks, her heart would have given a little twist in her chest and she'd have said kind of sadly that he was an old friend. Then she would have spent the rest of the day miserable, wondering where he was and if he was happy.

She'd never met anyone else like Nathan Banks. She'd never met anyone who'd pushed her, inspired her, challenged her and loved her like Nathan Banks.

Her life had seemed so settled. Her career plan had been in place. She had a nice place to stay and good work colleagues. But it wasn't enough. It would never be enough.

She'd met lots of nice guys. But no one she wanted to grow old with. No one she could still picture holding her hand when they were both grey-haired and wrinkled. That was how she'd always felt about Nathan. As if they were a perfect fit. As if they could last for ever. No one else would do.

Meeting Nathan again had made her realise just how much she was missing out. She craved him. Mentally, physically, spiritually. Being in the same room as him and not being able to have him was painful.

Why did she have to have cancer? Why did those horrible little cells have to replicate and cause damage in her body?

She winced. This was making her become a terrible person. The kind of person who wished cancer on someone else. She didn't want to be like that. She couldn't let herself be like that.

'Rachel?' Nathan was standing in front of her, holding the glass out towards her. His brow was creased as if he could see that something was wrong. The bubbles in the champagne tickled her nose. 'Are we going to toast the baby?' he asked, a little more warily.

She met his gaze full-on. Everything had just fallen into place for her. She couldn't be this person any more. 'No.'

He started and pulled the glass back, setting them both down on the table.

She braced herself to be hit by the wave of questions. Questions she had no idea how she would even begin to answer. But Nathan didn't ask any questions. He stepped forward and put his hands on her hips. She could feel the warmth of his fingers through the thin satin of her night-dress. His body was up against hers.

She was going to leave. She wanted to get away. So why did Nathan's body feel like an anchor against hers?

'Enough.' His voice was husky. 'Enough of this, Rachel. Eight years is too long. Eight years is far too long.' He reached up and gently stroked her cheek. 'I've missed you. I've felt lost without you. I need you to be with me. I need you to trust me again and know that I'll be here for you. I'm sorry you faced cancer alone.' He closed his eyes for a second. 'I'm sorry that for a whole host of mixed-up reasons you ended up on one side of the planet whilst I was on the other.' He gave his head a shake. 'I didn't know and I didn't understand.' His eyes fixed on hers. 'I now know about Darius. I don't know everything, and I don't need to know. But I do know why you have that tie to him. I feel as if I've spent the last eight years waiting for this moment—I just didn't know it. I need to move on. *We* need to move on. We don't get those eight years back again. I need to let things go, and so do you.' He slid his fingers through her hair. 'Otherwise,' he said throatily, 'we'll never get this. We'll spend the rest of our lives just drifting—not really living.' He pressed his head against hers. 'There's no way I'm letting you get on that boat without me. Not again, Rachel. Don't walk away from me again.'

He knew. He knew she planned to leave. But he hadn't come to shout at her. He'd held back. He'd given her some space. Had she really wanted to leave?

Her breath was stuck in her throat as she tried to strangle her sobs. She lifted her hands and placed them on his chest as she moved forward, letting her head rest on his shoulder. She could feel the beat of his heart beneath her palm. It was so familiar. It felt *so* right.

When they'd used to lie in bed together that was always how she would fall asleep—with her hand on his heart. It gave her comfort and reassurance and feeling it now was sending a wave of pulses throughout her body.

She couldn't lift her head. She couldn't look at him as she spoke. 'I love you,' she whispered. 'I've always loved you and I'll never stop.' Her hand moved upwards, along his jaw line with the day-old stubble she loved so much. She took a deep breath and lifted her head. 'I don't know why we ended up here together. Maybe it was some kind of twisted fate. I've been so confused these last few days, and there's only one thing I know for certain. I can't be the one to break you. I might have passed the five-year cancer-free mark. But it's not a guarantee. It's always there— always hanging over my head. I don't want to be sick around you, Nathan. I don't want you to have to nurse me. I don't want you to have to look after me.' She pressed her hand against her chest. 'And it's not because *I* would be sick. It's because of what it would do to *you*. I couldn't bear to see you like that. I couldn't watch you suffer.'

'And that's a reason? That's a reason not to have a chance to live our life together? That's a reason to run away again? Haven't you learned anything, Rach?' There was an edge to his voice, but he wasn't angry. He was incredulous.

'So you're going to spend the rest of your life hiding away? From life?' He threw up his hands. 'What if you never get cancer again, Rachel? What if the worst-case scenario just doesn't happen? Are you going to be sitting on your rocking chair wondering why you let life slip through your fingers?'

He stepped forward, his face right in front of hers. 'What if I get sick? What if *I* develop cancer? Would you walk away from me? Should I walk away from you because I don't want to see you upset? Don't you see how ridiculous that sounds?'

He put his hands on her shoulders. 'People take this leap every day, Rachel. When people commit to each other there's no guarantee of a happy ever after. You have to just take what life throws at you, and hope that you're strong enough to see each other through it.'

He put his hand on his chest. 'I believe we are, Rach. I believe we can be. I believe we should get our happy ever after. We've waited eight years for it. I don't want to wait a second longer.'

She was shaking. Her whole body was shaking now as the enormity of his words set in. This was what it felt like. This was what it felt like to have someone declare they would face anything for you. This was what she would have given anything to hear eight years ago—but she hadn't given him the chance.

He ran his hands down her arms. 'Don't walk away from this, Rach. Don't walk away again. That's the one thing that I can't take. Anything else I can face. Anything else I can face—with you by my side.'

She lifted her head as the tears streamed down her cheeks. He was smiling at her and she drank in every part of him. The weathered little lines around his eyes and mouth, the dark line of his stubble and the sincerity in his bright green eyes. She could spend an eternity looking at his face.

Her breathing was stuttering but her heartbeat felt steady. 'You've no idea how much I want this. I'm just so afraid.' Her voice was shaking. It felt like stepping off the side of a cliff into an abyss. There could be so much out there if you were willing to take the leap.

But Nathan had enough confidence for both of them. His smile widened and he held out his hand towards her. 'You don't have to be afraid, Rach. We're in this together. Every step of the way.'

His hand closed around hers. Warm, solid and reassuring. It sent a wave of heat up her arm.

'But what about everything else? Where will we stay? What about jobs? What will we do?'

He pulled her hard and fast against him. 'Let's take it one step at a time. The rest we'll figure out together.' One hand snaked through her hair and the other followed the curve of her satin night-dress. He whispered in her ear, his voice low, throaty and packed with emotion. 'What say we start at the very beginning and get a little reac-quainted?'

His bright green eyes were sparkling. It was like stepping back in time. And that look in his eyes sent the same quiver of anticipation down her spine that it always had.

Her lips danced across the skin on his shoul-ders, ending at the sensitive nape of his neck. Some things didn't change. 'I would very much like to get reacquainted with you, Dr Banks.'

He stepped back towards his bedroom and held out his hand towards her. It was the first time she'd felt certainty in eight long years. She reached out and grabbed it and let him lead her to her happy ever after—no matter what it con-tained.

EPILOGUE

One year later

RACHEL WAS PACING. Her nerves were jangling and her heart was thudding in her chest, the swoosh of her cream wedding gown the only noise in the quiet bathroom.

Nathan reached over and grabbed her hand, pulling her towards him. He smiled as he settled one hand on her lace-covered waist and lifted the other to touch one of the little brown curls of her carefully coiffed hair.

'Anyone would think you were nervous,' he said, clearly feeling no nerves.

'Of course I'm nervous. I feel sick.' She looked back towards the sink. 'What time is it?'

He shook his head. 'Be patient, Rachel. We have all the time in the world for this.' He gestured his head towards the door. 'Our guests will think I'm in here trying to talk my bride out of her cold feet.'

Rachel sucked in a deep breath. 'Oh, no.' Her hand flew up to the sweetheart neckline of her dress. 'That is what they'll think, isn't it?' She broke from his grasp for a few seconds as she paced again, then stepped over and placed her hands on his chest, her sincere brown eyes fixing on his. 'You know I'd never get cold feet about marrying you. This is the surest I've ever been about anything in my entire life.'

He leaned forward and dropped a soft kiss on her pink lips. 'I know that,' he said. He looked over her shoulder. 'If the celebrant catches me kissing the bride before we say "I do" we might be in trouble.'

She nodded nervously. 'Is it time yet? Is it time?'

He glanced at his watch again, then took her hand in his. 'You know, I don't want you to be disappointed if it's not what you hoped. I'm marrying the woman that I love. I want our day to be about you and me and the fact we're committing to a life together.'

'I know that, I know that. But I just can't help thinking that there has to be another reason for my late period. It can't just be the stress of the wedding.'

He laughed. 'I don't think a wedding car driver has ever had to stop for a pregnancy test before. You nearly gave him a heart attack.'

She squeezed her eyes shut for a second. 'You look—I can't.'

Her head was spinning. They'd planned their wedding in the space of a few months. In less than two weeks they would be back in the UK, both in new jobs nearer to Charlie, Nathan's brother. She was to start training as a GP, and Nathan to start his training as a surgeon. He was already cracking jokes about being the oldest surgeon in town.

She'd always worried that her cancer treatment would have affected her fertility. Nathan had known that when he'd asked her to marry him. *Families can be made up in many ways.* Those had been his words. He was more concerned about not missing out on another eight years with the woman he loved.

Nathan took a step forward and glanced at the white stick.

She clenched her fists. She couldn't bear the waiting. 'One line or two?'

His eyes widened and his face broke into a smile as he grabbed her and lifted her up, spinning her around in the cramped bathroom at the courthouse. 'Two.'

'What?' She couldn't believe it. Not today.

He was still spinning her and she put her hands around his neck as he gently lowered her to the floor. 'So, are you ready? Are you ready to make me the happiest man on the planet, Mrs Banks?'

She rested her head on his shoulder as things started to sink in. 'Mrs Banks. Oh, wow. This day can't get any better, can it?'

There was a twinkle in his green eyes. 'Oh, I think it can.' He picked up her bouquet of pink roses that had been abandoned next to the sink and handed them to her. 'Let's settle our guests' nerves. They'll think we're not coming back out.'

There was a knock on the door and Charlie stuck his head in. 'Are you two okay? Freddie has already dropped the rings off that cushion twice. If he does it again you can find them.'

Charlie's little girl, Matilda, was their pink-gowned flower girl and Freddie, his little boy, was their pageboy.

Nathan gave Rachel a wink. 'Sorry, Charlie, it seems we've got some news.' He intertwined his fingers with hers. 'It seems that two are about to become three.'

It took a few seconds for the news to click, then Charlie's eyes widened. 'What?' He crossed the bathroom in two strides, enveloping Rachel in a bear hug. 'Fabulous. I can't wait to meet my new niece or nephew.' He stepped back. 'Wait—is this a secret; can we tell anyone?'

They glanced at each other, Rachel's hand automatically going to her stomach. 'We need to wait, don't we? We need to get it confirmed?'

Nathan picked up the pregnancy test. 'We've already done that. Let's tell the world, Rachel. Let's tell them just how good life's about to get.' He winked. 'We'll just get married first.'

She nodded and took a deep breath.

Charlie led her over to the door. 'Now, let's get

this show on the road. I've still to make you my sister-in-law.' He gave her a kiss on the cheek as he disappeared outside.

Nathan turned to face her. 'Your dad will be having a heart attack out there. Are you ready?'

She nodded. 'I've never been more ready.' She smoothed down the front of her dress and took a quick check in the mirror to straighten her veil. She'd embraced the whole pink theme for her wedding. Her cream satin and lace dress had a deep pink sash in the middle, matching her bouquet and the few scattered roses in her hair. Nathan had obligingly worn a pink shirt and tie and had the same coloured rose in his lapel. All for her.

Nathan walked out first and she joined her nervous-looking father. He'd been so happy when he'd found out she and Nathan were moving back to London. It had been an easy decision to make. They'd stayed and worked in Australia for another ten months before talking about plans for the future. Both of them agreed they'd like to be closer to Charlie, and she'd been over the moon when Nathan had proposed to her at Darius's wedding a few months before. They'd decided both things at once—to find jobs back in England and plan their wedding.

Her dad held out his arm. 'Everything okay?'

She gave him her widest smile. 'Everything's perfect, Dad, and it's going to get even more so.'

His brow furrowed curiously as he glanced towards the doors of the courthouse just as they were opened by the staff. Nathan and Charlie went in first.

She smiled and her stomach gave a little flip-flop. Eight years ago she'd thought her life was about to end—now, it was just beginning.

As the sun streamed through the windows Rachel walked in on her father's arm to join the man that she loved.

Her husband. Her baby's father.

Her fate.

* * * * *